SLUM GOD BILLIONAIRE

BANASMITA BARUAH

INDIA • SINGAPORE • MALAYSIA

ISBN 979-8-89133-919-4

REVIEW FROM WORLD FAMOUS VIOLINIST
"DimaTkachenko"

Thank you for the opportunity to get acquainted with you and your new book.

You have done an excellent job depicting various aspects of human life in a way that stands out and is hard to match. Congratulations!

All the best wishes
Dima Tkachenko

* * * * *

London
9 January 2024

Banasmita has excelled herself in her maiden adventure in literature world by penning Slum God Billionaire. Her story leads us deeper into the reality of human existence full of challenges.

It is a fantastic read. I am from Thomas Hardy's West Country area I can say that Banasmita's style is Hardy like profound and realistic.

John Dawer
Lecturer in Philosophy

Contents

Acknowledgement

Love, inspiration, support and encouragement are synonymous with footprints in a scale to 'success.' My writing career would not have been possible without the much needed gadgets namely the persons in my life who have been the source of inspiration and constant encouragement, thus trying evermore to give this writing journey a 'name.'

My mother-in law had never ceased to encourage me till her last breath. My father-in law only waits to hear my success story.

Most importantly my husband Mr.Rajib has been supporting me from day one of our marriage. How can I close this chapter without mentioning about my parents, Dr Dimbeswar Baruah and Dr. Dharma Prabha Baruah, their support is immense. Again my brother Mr. Bikash, my sons Pivrat and Krithvik, their love is bountiful.

Friends are the most prized possessions on earth. I am indeed blessed to have a gem of friends who with their untiring efforts tried to give this novel a 'finishing touch.' Shefali Upadhyay, Kaveri Prasad, Namrata Thapa, Aadrika Singh, Maria Robledo, Shafiqa Shaikh are some of my many friends aiding me in the enhancements of the plots of this novel.

I am ever indebted to one and all.

Disclaimer

This is a work of fiction. All the names, characters, places, events, organisations and incidents in this book are either the product of the author's imagination or used in a fictitious manner. Any resemblance to actual persons, living or dead, or actual events is purely coincidental.

Witch

Life's Journey during corona is a plethora of unimaginable circumstances. Uncertainty reigned supreme at every second, every minute, and every hour.

Armed with an unconquerable mind and amidst greater despondency, the protagonist Bhoomi had lived life alive and gave it a significance that was adorned with an unnamed newness.

We are the people on the planet of slums
We strive to survive in this perilous drive
We live under the same roof, with inconsistencies abound
We try to find small happiness in the worst of circumstances around
Hungry eyes, empty stomach still, we find a kind of security
We are the emblem of friendliness and hospitality.

The monotonous lives of the people needed no mention. Pangs of separation had led to endless tragedies as death, the ultimate truth, had embraced many a world population. Fear of death was rampant, however, portrayed here as a virus less dangerous than human beings.

Bhoomi repeatedly tried to prove her grandma, Shantibai as right in every life proceedings. Her teachings had matured her in the ways of this world. "Not knowing what life has in treasure, we need to move with careful measure." That was the simple belief of Bhoomi until the end.

We are God's creation, and now our every craze lies in becoming one as the creator, a saviour of mankind.

Suspending all negative emotions and traversing on routes laid with positivism was undoubtedly a closet of abundant merriment and love. Diverse incidents a man had to face, but in the long run, he who could thwart it with a courageous stunt would only survive the lives confront.

Slum dwellers are gods indeed with a lot more wonderful souls lurking around its cosmos.

A small lane of a New Delhi's slum, *Purbi Bagh* were full of vibrant voices. Rising from its midst was an innocent soul whose indistinct voice had the air of mixed feelings. Tired of the harsh ways of life, Bhoomi sometimes got dejected and was torn immensely. Again, her people herein had loved her enough that she could not live without mentioning about them, her friends and neighbours alike. At the same time, Bhoomi never forgot to appreciate her grandma for her intricate and fatiguing labour without which her life would have been synonymous with the uttermost tear. Taking every day as a newer chapter of life, its manifold twists only enhanced her life to an extended horizon that remained worth a phase.

The gruesome ways of Shantibai, who had raised her granddaughter, Bhoomi, had never ceased to hurt her enormously. Her despotic ways were simply intolerable. In a desperate bid to decode the meaning of life, Bhoomi said words which simply invoked pity.

I mourned for my desperate condition,
I know little of my grandma's love and affection.
I long for my lost days,
Though I know the golden hues of my earlier days will never come back.

Bhoomi had hardly a perception of her earlier years as she had lost her parents when she was four years old, and since then, her short-statured granny was her only constant aid. A silent realisation dawned, "Excessive brooding over the past results in nothing. Life and its manifold twists only strengthens my life to face and withstand hurdles whatsoever."

Bhoomi slowly walked into an unknown arena. She soothed her mind and soon lost herself in imagination, and this time, the small ponderings had lulled her into a deep slumber. It was a hot sunny day with peepal trees all around as if synonymous with shades of protection. Meanwhile, she had a short knap; waking up, she found herself in a cottage nearby. Gaurilal and his wife reassured her of the safer abode and, in simple words, narrated the reason for bringing her to their house. Meena, Gaurilal's wife said in a grave tone that a witch had been at large and warned Bhoomi of the impending danger. They gave her a five hundred note, and Bhoomi's gloomy face eclipsed briefly. Unknown faces though, Bhoomi could see 'sharing and caring' attitude in them.

The money can bring a smile in my grandma's face.
Almighty knows the woes and keeps us safer from foes.

She rhymed her words in a manner that signified her abundant maturity. Gaurilal's wife assured her of never-ending help, as the childless couple could see their child in her. The farewell note came as a great succour when life's turbulences had shaken her to an unimaginable vortex. Indeed the whole day had become a memorable episode for Bhoomi.

The greener world is always green; it is we who cannot view it clearer.

The anticipation of a bright future came as a positive source of inspiration to Bhoomi, who had learned to leave the past in the past, leaving it possibly many yards.

As evening fell, Shantibai got enveloped with a kind of peculiar restlessness. Her face had worn a forlorn look. Sooner the realisation came, her granddaughter would reach the corridor in no time energized her manifold.

Inquisitiveness arose, seeing Bhoomi pale and worn out.

Shantibai wondered what could have ailed her granddaughter.

Seeing Shantibai, Bhoomi had burst into tears. When narrated, Shantibai tightly held her in her arms at once, giving a braver look, concealing the fear within, as to Bhoomi 'witch' was an unheard story altogether. The fantasy world of Bhoomi had never welcomed dark elements whatsoever. Shantibai thought it proper to give her some slices of reality; thus, embracing her in her arms, introduced Bhoomi to the story of 'the old witch and her two sisters,' which had unnerved her.

Shantibai paused, and in order to remove the dread she added, "Witch, and witchcraft are the manifestations of an illogical mind. It is largely unreal and open to personal interpretation. An empowered mind never falls prey to such false practises and impractical doctrines."

Again, she gave Bhoomi a slight insight into the very subject of alcoholism, how it had eaten into the vitals of our society. Bhoomi could recollect last week's incident in the neighbouring bye-lanes of how young and old menfolk enacted and exhibited the worst phase of human nature.

In greater desperation, Bhoomi blasted "Grandma, you are right. It's evil, none should rest until we can wipe out this devil."

I cursed my state to know the world at large. I am too late.

Good and bad people exist, absolute biasedness is what I should not enlist.

'Lady luck' had favoured them as Gaurilal's wife handed over a five hundred rupee to Bhoomi as a farewell note of love.

"The childless couple could visualises their progeny in me as they applaud me for my rather amiable and soft-spoken nature.," Bhoomi said in a humble manner to her grandma.

The salty tears of Shantibai were manifold to hold, but she took Bhoomi in her grip once more, uttering the words, "I am the worst grandma; I am the one who can hardly earn and give solace to my little soul." Shantibai became desperate realising that she may not be able to fulfill her goals.

My grandma has a soft corner but is hidden.

It was as if Shantibai, pre-occupied with the idea of protection, gave her a light warning; "Strangers are always strangers with whom we need to be alert, seeing abundance, our eyes should never get blurred." Saying this, Shantibai retired to her somewhat hardened bed.

The night slowly enveloped the whole sky as if the busy old day was put to rest. Bhoomi grew suspicious of the intentions of the night sky, whether its design was to give some tranquil or a night with something mischievous to happen. Bhoomi closed her eyes as if trying to end the day's uncanny happenings.

The cold, imaginative world was the usual refuge where I can heave a sigh of relief and find a home, a dreamland, or a safe recluse.

She dreamt of the fairies hopping and jumping, imploring her to sleep with their soft and sweet melodious tunes. The soothing dreams were those farfetched images that transformed her into a girl where her life got the entire fulfillment.

However, by bouts of ill luck, that night was the same usual night, and the dreadful nature of her dreams has made her world rather fearsome. Thunderstorms uprooting trees, thatched roofs of the houses falling, and voices of women screaming aloud suddenly brought Bhoomi into the real murky world.

Alas, where can I breathe?
Where can I have a protective retreat?
It was as if dream had refused to give her a safer embrace.

The natural and imaginative world entered into a clash. Betrayed by the two worlds, Bhoomi needed guidance about where to find meaning in life. A silent understanding emerged.

Better or bitter, life has to be lived somehow; an escapist attitude will only dampen my spirits to encounter real-life hurdles.

This world and the other worlds are not a good place to live though.

Hoping that a better word was on her way, Bhoomi started viewing variegated hues and shades of hope, trying to encompass in it a broader vision. She believed hope could kindle her dampened spirit.

Spirits high or low is only momentary
My inner strength and hope will but grow perpetually.

Bhoomi's mental strength in the face of direst circumstances was a notable feature of her character. She braved nature's forces, giving it a tough fight by ousting all the opposing forces and installing a positive belief system as the only armament to stand by her in the darkest hours.

A girl, though not mature enough to handle the affairs of this world, was inwardly able to say 'no' to her grandma's stories. Bhoomi believed that 'witch' was non-existent. It was only the result of misconceptions and false assumptions among people. *Longer these misconceptions exist, the sooner it will signal a dark era of humanity.*

Again, Shanti Bai proudly proclaimed that slum life is a thing of divine beauty, countless mishaps could not dampen their spirits as accepting reality has become their forte. By braving any untoward circumstances, they tried to challenge the facts of life with a renewed vigour and a reinvigorating spirit that was hitherto unknown.

Purbi Bagh

The slums were one of the worst-hit areas during this fateful time of covid 19. Lack of proper sanitation, accommodation, and overpopulation had led many to fall into its death trap. Indeed, 'life and death' was just a bridge apart. Sometimes, they became so close to each other that the line of separation had almost become extinct. Those few surviving had learned a great lesson, 'Death is a great leveller,' and that 'human physiology is the same for one and all'. Acceptability had become an innate nature of humanity.

Sitting on the veranda, Shantibai wondered what had saddened her mind was the sanitation problem in her area and how it had become a significant challenge for women in slums. Bhoomi had a changed view of her grandma.

My grandma's hostile ways are laid with a purpose.

Strictness coupled with love generated a different kind of emotion altogether.

We, the slum dwellers, are forbidden to dream anything better.

Life's canvass has been thrilling, at times humiliating, and further, by transporting life to a phase of divine tranquillity, it gets encompassed with an undefined dilemma. The bond of 'life within life' is torn by ghastly figures.

Temptation aside, Bhoomi fortified herself to set a new definition of life. Thus, embarking on a unique plane of vision, Bhoomi geared her paths in the most righteous way ever imagined. Her feeble look attracted the attention of her grandma.

Shantibai wondered, "Such a harsh look from Bhoomi has never been seen, I wonder if I could have been much stronger, I would have given her a carefree life."

It marked her ultimate love for her grandchild. Shantibai had a motherly affection for the young girls and ladies. They endeared her to a degree that was hardly unsurpassable. Corona times were brutal she could understand how bereft of hygienic ways her people would suffer a lot. To give life a smooth sail, she never forgot some rejoicings with her granddaughter. Bhoomi derived a peculiar satisfaction by distributing delicacies with her wonderful neighbours as well. Indeed, it was not a slum but a resort with many blessed souls herein.

The money Gaurilal's wife gave was in Bhoomi's safe reserves. However, Bhoomi decided to hand over the cash to grandma, as it would be the best option if the money had to be safe. Shantibai was not happy at the outset receiving the cash from Bhoomi. However, she accepted, as it would encourage her granddaughter to 'work for life.' She was happy that Bhoomi's good etiquette had impressed everyone to a polite conclusion.

Grandma, I owe my life to you, your actions such kind and selfless ones, have taught me many lessons of worldly wisdom.

At best, Bhoomi's thinking's were sincere in that she realised the immense labour and toil that Shantibai had taken to nurture her.

"You are my promise, to give you the best life is what I shall never cease." Such utterings only pointed that Shantibai was too serious in life-related matters. Bhoomi replied in a softer tone, "I hardly have words to convey my innumerable thanks to you, I realise you are my parents in lieu."

Nature had matured Bhoomi in the light of enlightened knowledge. She had never visited a school, but as if the angels in the kingdom of God had given her immense education.

I rejoice when my grandma smiles
This way, I can cross wonderfully few more miles.

Bhoomi said a few lines to her grandma that only expressed her immense maturity, "My Grandma, you compromise at every step. Not that you willingly accept your much allotted fate, you struggle but circumstances are such that you see no other alternative. You are caught up in the role conflicts of being a grandmother and a home maker. I love you a lot."

Bhoomi relished the mouth savouring dishes. It was a special day, as Shantibai's usual grumbling nature was eclipsed behind her smiles. Even her neighbours joined them in that small party without trying to ask about the significance of the small gathering. The previous night's dream gave Bhoomi a frightening experience. Still, the day's rejoicing made Bhoomi oblivious of earlier happenings. Her life had gained momentum from her spirited thinking, making her unmindful of what misfortunes had befallen her.

Smiling face signals the advent of something bigger and greater. I smile and like to see the world smile. I feel earth has the beauties of a child.

Bhoomi's momentary presumptions got embedded with abundant innocence that vanished sooner with encountering grave realities of life. Shantibai had no regular income; the occasional meals and the utter helplessness are the usual phenomena seen by Bhoomi since the early days of childhood. Seeing her grandma tying a piece of cloth in her belly was a never-missed situation that brought incessant tears to her mind. Life unfolding the worst chapters of life at such a tender age gave her tears an unknown definition, a way to quench her thirst in a different plane altogether.

Consoling grandma, Bhoomi told, "Inner mental confidence can only help to withstand life's brutalities, which is caused by absolute poverty."

Hearing this, Shantibai heaved a sigh of relief, thinking worldly education had given her granddaughter a kind of 'superb enlightenment'. Bhoomi added the word 'hurry', which guides the modern world.

Bhoomi pondered and murmured again to her grandma, "Hasty actions lead to tension and insecurity, man does not hesitate to take it as a safer guide. But the disastrous consequences are apparent. May be the sense of belonging nowhere, haunts him resulting many to perish in the void. They might miss the right inspiration and proper channelisation."

Shantibai was taken aback by the abundant wisdom in her granddaughter's closet when Bhoomi quietly said, "There seems to be such a surge of activities that the more one divides his interests and allegiances, the less time one has for living. Understanding oneself is time-consuming, preventing one from understanding life's meaning."

Shantibai voiced and further added, "Dealing a situation with dynamism and foresight is synonymous with a life free of stress."

These small lessons and interchange of ideas made their lives worth living especially for Bhoomi, who had seen this natural world through the lens of her grandma. She retired to her bed with a warmer disposition.

Divine never gives us an onus that we cannot fulfil.

A Farewell to Kusum Devi

Shantibai's words resounded the immense love she had nursed for her granddaughter. Bhoomi sat cross legged in a cot that was laid in the ground. She started pondering on life issues.

Devoid of an external controlling power, channelising medium, life comes to an abrupt halt at a wrong end. It is a desperate situation in which crisis gets overloaded and heralds either a total doomsday or a new beginning. Man has an inner voice, inner sense of justification and he should analyse everything not in a hot heated impulsive manner but with a cool mind seeing that the interests of the society is not hampered.

Occasional joys of learning new dogmas had helped Bhoomi adjust to her grandma's variegated tides.

Shantibai wanted discipline to prevail in one's life and would never tolerate any upheaval. It simply pointed to Shantibai's utmost concern for her granddaughter. Shantibai was never dogmatic about any religion. Though she had no formal education, Shantibai could read a newspaper, implying she had a knack for learning. Reading out news to Bhoomi was a simple way to widen her mental horizon, thereby bestowing a broader view of life. Her benign request to Bhoomi was to stay away from petty religious issues and said in simple words to Bhoomi, "Man needs a faith, which is reasonable full of ethical convictions, a faith to which the disoriented mind must cling to for the disciplining of his inward nature, so that he doesn't collapse even in the face of disastrous defeat. The perfect blending of life and religion could only be rightly manifested in the great epics stories."

It was a hot day with a hot summer breeze sweeping the floors of their thatched house. The cool moralising had helped Bhoomi to remain unmindful of the heat wave outside. Sitting near the broken windowpanes, she was visualizing different living phenomena in variegated shapes of clouds. It only proved she had all the innocence of a child coupled with imaginative powers richly manifested. This way, Bhoomi guarded her pleasures very cautiously and kept them beyond the reach of friends and foes alike.

The clouds with their different hues and shapes
It has made it seem great
Oh! have I the wings of a bird
I could be one on their chart.

These beautiful reflections of Bhoomi indeed pointed to the beauties of a sinless mind. Bhoomi transported herself to the world of reality. She learned that she had to toil in the house of a wealthy businessman. This news brought her mixed feelings and said, "Grandma, I know you are happy at my new job, but the pain of leaving you the whole day is simply unbearable."

Shantibai blessed her so that she could withstand any storm. Bhoomi believed that human beings only make the journey of a thousand miles possible with a few softening voices.

The happy events became overshadowed by the demise of Shantibai's bosom friend, Kusum Devi. She was the only friend with whom Shantibai would share life's more comfortable and unhappy facts. For a moment, Shantibai was speechless; she was unable to cry. Bhoomi thought it might have an adverse effect on her grandma's health. Bhoomi gave a slight remembrance of the happy days Shantibai spent with Kusumdevi and how she stood by her in the most precarious moments.

Bhoomi uttered, "Grandma, Kusum Devi is the only friend with whom you could share the luminous and darker phases of your life chapters. Now she is no more." There was a momentary state of disbelief. Bhoomi was worried about her grandmother, who tried to recollect and make Shantibai remember the whirlwinds of her life, the time when Kusum Devi had stood beside her.

Bhoomi whispered in her rather melancholy voice and said, "Grandma, stillness will only bring health hazard, life on earth is already measured."

All efforts proved futile.

Bhoomi still did not cease to give a last try and mouthed, "The fact that you have now lost the world, your son who was the only support in your old age had left you untimely too; you are still alive only because of the constant mental support given by Kusum Devi. Now that she is dead, where will you go to seek advice or consolation?"

Shantibai at once burst into tears. She cried aloud and fell into the arms of Bhoomi. She held her tightly and repeatedly asked her never to leave her in the lurch.

"I am there, Grandma, do not worry

That she is no more. I feel sorry

But you have taught me this is life

So even through life's worst circumstances, we have to survive."

This little consoling word came from the mouth of Bhoomi. Shantibai for a moment, could not believe it.

"Little but mature and wise, earlier I thought of you as naughty and full of lies," Shantibai softly articulated.

Shantibai's earlier conception of Bhoomi took a slight transformation, and she remained in her grandma's closet throughout the night.

A Visit to a Sai Temple

A new day emerged and Shantibai was as usual restless in imparting newer lessons to her granddaughter. Religion, though an eight letter word was abound with more serious connotations. Religious bigotry, fanaticism had eaten into the very roots of a society, if not properly guarded could lead to disastrous consequences. Shantibai gave a brilliant presentation to Bhoomi, "Religious tolerance is almost a lost word in this earthly abode. We all live together in the colony. We should remember we are with people from different regions, religions, and castes, all living nearby. At one time, it might also create animosity. We should handle people and their sentiments very carefully. Modern man feels himself rootless as he is unaware of his real self. He is completely occupied in the changes and chances of mere existence. Reality can be encountered only by those who have attained integration and harmony by overcoming the conflict within themselves."

Shantibai took Bhoomi to the Sai Baba temple nearby not knowing that Bhoomi regularly visited it in the noontime. It was a place where she could breathe the air of harmony. Bhoomi could see the Gyan Darshan program in the T.V., hear religious discourses from various *gurumatas*. Shantibai tried her best to make her granddaughter acquire the best of social knowledge. She thanked *gurumatas* for acting as a pathfinder to her granddaughter.

Just then, three transgenders started distributing food outside the temple. It was an unusual scene. Many times, Bhoomi came across so-called *hijras*. Their stylistic way of approaching fascinated Bhoomi. The smell of their elegant perfumes, red coloured lipsticks with bright *bindis* hardly failed to capture her attention. Bhoomi came down the stairs and lovingly accepted the food as she had been without food since morning. Unlike others, Shantibai, too, accepted gladly without prompting a single word. Some boys came and threw the plates of these *hijras* a few minutes later, mocking them untiringly.

Fierce fighting followed, and Bhoomi grew evermore curious. Shantibai explained, "How these sections of people face constant social discrimination and that cases of ill–treatment, cruelty, and violence these people face get neglected. Their plight only gets a silent answer. The transgender community has been shunned by society and excluded from education and employment. Parents tend to abandon them after birth, and nothing can be more tragic as they consider keeping a transgender person at home as most dishonourable."

"Are there no laws to punish these unruly boys, grandma?" Shantibai replied in the affirmative, saying somewhere in the newspaper she read, a person could be jailed from six months to one or two years if one was found abusing a transgender community person. Bhoomi shouted at the ferocious boys, saying 'go back' outrageously and that they could not escape the police. Bhoomi cried in utter dismay at the ways of this world, "I am angry, I am shattered, maybe I am revengeful; I would show them my anguish is real and hateful."

The earth belongs to all
Mistreating the transgender will lead them to a drastic fall.
Accepting all mankind on earth in a righteous way
Will only bring about a harmonious existence, is what I say.

Shantibai, though frightened, was very happy to see the unusual valour in her well-raised granddaughter. Shantibai was pretty apprehensive that the curses of *hijras* were from the bosom of their painful hearts. Curses arising from their painful afflictions could have dangerous consequences according to Shantibai. Likewise, their blessings were powerful too. Births and other ceremonies were attended by them without announcing their arrival. Bhoomi believed in fear of receiving curses from them, people wholeheartedly pay for their services, though mostly uninvited.

Thus, a slice of society got a realistic depiction from the scenes recently visited. Bhoomi cried aloud seeing their plight.

It was about the *hijras* living in Delhi, a life led by them in isolation, shame, stigma, and social exclusion, and for whom justice would always remain a farfetched word.

The search for peace and harmony cannot be in a secluded place or a well-built temple. Our mind is a reservoir of peace and tranquillity; we are how we channel our thoughts.

Bhoomi was happy that God had given her a house full of wisdom. Shantibai thought the dangerous world would not be so tricky for Bhoomi if her mind remained in the righteous way. Shantibai saw that every chapter of her granddaughter's life was ennobled with incredible moral lessons, so much so that her later life would not depend on her.

Late in the evening, as they reached home, total darkness encircled them. The solar powered lamps installed in their narrow lane got stolen again. In utter desperation Bhoomi murmured, "We slum dwellers have been deprived of all facilities. Bereft of security, housing durability, and water scarcity, this is no lesser than hell."

Still, I want to hang on here as slum life has given me a sense of community and belonging. This solidarity has helped my grandma and her neighbours on various issues.

Bhoomi's heart hardened seeing tears in her grandma's eyes.

Weary, my grandma becomes early in the morn
I wish I would have never been born
With starvation deprivation, we are always adorned.
We symbolise a maze of poverty, a myriad of struggling humanity
Amidst perfect agony, we learn to smile though
In streets where happiness seems almost buried
Still, that laughter and love, fierce wind cannot dry it.

Bhoomi had that positive vibe that could not be dethroned by any circumstances whatsoever and which had rebuilt her stamina evermore. Bhoomi's state of mind became unstable when she herself had pronounced a negative view of the world that it was marching towards a dangerous future.

We are aware of living in a tragic age where evil forces reign supreme
One conflict clears the way for another.
Irrational feelings, sufferings, intrigues, plots, counterplots make of them
A seething mass of mysterious and unpredictable events.

Shantibai was happy to see Bhoomi, marching ahead towards enlightenment.

Shantibai uttered, "The cosmic forces reside in every individual as an entity. It is this inner presence which empowers our senses to act as they do. Caught in the turbulence of life at an emotional keel man needs an external guiding force to rise above himself?"

Bhoomi was recording in her memory every letter, every word of her grandma.

I am flushed with happiness seeing my grandma, my biggest pathfinder in my life.

A silence once again prevailed when Shantibai opined, "The youths are on the threshold of a new destructive spirit. They live on plane of ideas rather than reason. 'Chastity' the most valued word has lost all its significance. The youths have reached such a demoralised state that it becomes quite difficult to make good come back."

It was almost 10 pm and Bhoomi was about to fall in her grandma's lap. Shantibai took a short break and prepared a small dinner and the tiresome day came to an end.

Diwali Vibes

Sounds of imperturbable happiness
Wonders of humans are countless
Flavour of foods ripening in tranquillity
Light caressing fingers are creating an unparalleled visual gallery.

Every year since childhood, Bhoomi waited eagerly for the 'Diwali'. Its advent was a joyous moment for her as she thought the devils got their final exit on that day.

All dark powers get a tag of annihilation

As Earth gets the badge of illumination.

Shantibai used to narrate the story of Ramayana, a kind-hearted king who left his kingdom and lived in exile for fourteen years. It was in the forest where Ravana took Sita away from Rama. Rama's ire reached the verge of frenzy and finally defeated Ravana. Diwali is celebrated to welcome Rama and Sita along with Laxmana to Ayodhya.

"With houses getting dilapidated, can there be ultimate solace?" Bhoomi shouted in utter desperation.

Bhoomi could remember not saving a single pie to buy a new cooking utensil during *dhanteras.*

My prayers for Lakshmi puja is simple
We are the unfortunate lot; all look at us and giggle
Perhaps present fate is the result of our previous birth's folly
A promise to make this life holy.
We need a little prosperity that is on you, 'Goddess' solely.

Bhoomi lighted a small earthen lamp and filled it with oil on the night of the new moon to invite the presence of Lakshmi, the goddess of wealth. Bhoomi lighted two lamps, one for Mother Earth too, to whom an incurable corona disease had descended. With positivity in her mind, Bhoomi fell into her grandma's lap. The incident of an acid attack on a girl, which grandma read to her, shook her to an immeasurable degree.

Acid attack is one of the most heinous offenses on a woman. Bhoomi tried to suspend all emotions temporarily.

Shantibai was having a murky look seeing Mother Earth in a perilous situation, "Oh! I feel disoriented reading news about evil existence thus, making me electrically fused."

Shantibai once again regained her earlier self and tried to infuse the highest positivism in Bhoomi by participating in the Diwali festival though in a smaller manner. Shantibai fed her hungry mind with lessons for future and pronounced," Diwali and firecrackers go hand in hand.

The Diwali nights bedazzle with an array of sparkling lights. The endless bursting of crackers mark the advent of Diwali. Fireworks are a blend of gunpowder and other ingredients that explode with loud noises, accompanied by colourful sparks and flames. The emission of harmful gases give rise to many complicated problems in the human body. It increases the risk of asthma, lung and heart diseases. Lighting *diyas* is always a safer way to celebrate this festival of light."

Bhoomi silently and carefully preserved and treasured in her mind another chapter of her life that was worth a lesson for one and all.

1ˢᵗ January

The reality of life was too harsh for Bhoomi. No relief or respite from any side was the hardest thing Bhoomi had to encounter. Seeing grandma's ailing condition became a sight quite unbearable for Bhoomi. She could not prove to be a pacifying balm in her distressed condition. Bhoomi had no other alternative but to rush to a new job site. A week had lapsed, but she could not revisit her more unexplored destination.

The world can be even better
The dualities only point to something greater
A balance phenomenon rather
Has made our earth a place for harmonies to gather.

The most important thing in life is the unity underlying our life and the realisation that the insensitivity to our fellow creature is the external manifestation of the disunity embedded in our consciousness. One way to achieve peace of mind is to practice spiritual discipline, which will transform us. The sense of divisiveness agitating our mind will begin to mend long-standing feelings of disharmony, and give us a tremendous sense of security.

Bhoomi's deep inner knowledge and wisdom helped her to sustain life's variegated tests and even exposed her to the outside world. Extreme poverty has made the school door forever shut for her.

World is my school. Every day is my lesson. Such a painful realisation did not break down the morale of Bhoomi. She pronounced, "All experiences are nothing but making me bold enough to face the world from every standpoint."

*I grow up without knowing what school is
Though I know the world teacher will not make me a fool.*

Placing her foot on the natural soil gave her every page of life a different significance worth remembering.

Somewhere down the lane, the New Year bells had made her exuberant. However, covid protocols had forbidden great get-togethers. From childhood, Shantibai had never missed an opportunity to welcome the New Year dazzlingly. On its eve, Shantibai was quite woebegone thinking that many lives would pass away in the coming year if the virus became vibrant. Seeing grandma in a melancholy mood over the untoward happening on earth, Bhoomi tried to make a slight digression as if nothing ailed mother earth. She was overly curious to hear the world news, which she thought her grandma had never missed. Bhoomi had memorised her speech a month before. On the 1st of January, with some divine invocations, Shantibai started the day with chanting long mantras hardly knowing her granddaughter had well coped with the ways of this world. Family astrologer had come and predicted a bright future for Bhoomi and foretold things which Shantibai could not even digest. She voiced, "I hear world news but panditji says my Bhoomi will soon be in the world news." Shantibai's words implied that she was an optimist but well kept her foot on earth.

The onset of New Year is the beckoning call for something new, abandoning older subdued feelings of hatred animosity and encompassing within its fold a somewhat lost terminology called oneness. The diversity of the human mind looms large, leading to the large-scale mental degeneration of humankind. Regarding a mass movement towards more incredible human goodness and understanding, oneness is the only way to create many revolutionary ideas to eliminate cosmic chaos.

Expressing thoughts above, Bhoomi was superbly happy that wise words overflowed her mouth when she said, "The human mind has become a vacuum, giving every unwanted element a free pass. Rediscovering within oneself the power to realize one's potential and visualise and realise one's dreams will give life a reason to live. But the strenuous effort seems to go in vain when one sees the outside world enveloped with deadly terror."

Shantibai's inquest on life was remarkable when she shared, "Lack of self-judgment leads one to be dictated by other's terms. The imposition of another's will on us automatically takes from us the power of self-analysis, the ability to examine the situation from our point of view."

The worldly-wise talks filled their stomach much more than little quota of food they consumed.

Bhoomi's loitering mind murmured, "Before judging, we should have that compatible attitude to discuss our ideas' pros and cons with other experienced members of society. The submissive attitude doesn't lower us but instead uplifts us in the eyes of those who bowed down in the same way, knowing that submission only helps us to be more experienced from a knowledge point of view."

Patience is the foremost thing we should possess to analyse
ourselves,
We shouldn't lose courage in considering our imperfections
But instantly set about remedying them.

Bhoomi believed we should contribute to the enhancement of peace which, if we can understand, peace could never cease. Bhoomi spoke on 'New Year' which even panditji was shocked and was immensely happy that his prediction would come true one day. Shantibai in the heart of hearts could visualise a bright future for her granddaughter.

Bhoomi had nothing to give but hoped her long speech full of knowledgeable texts would be praised by her grandma. She knew about her grandma's fragile health and that she might not endure too long. No wonder she paused, leaving aside what had gone and what would come, as for Bhoomi, the 'present is the best moment to be cherished.'

OCD

The trauma of living a life full of insecurities and restlessness instead of rekindling one's spirit dampens it to an unending extent. Again, a breakdown can be the beginning of a breakthrough wherein living amidst trauma prepares us for a life of radical transformation. The wave of newness is like a rejuvenating tonic that will make one oblivious of everything that was wanted or unwanted, thus paving the way from a bleak present to a better future.

Bhoomi believed the known and unknown elements merged in one's life, making our life somewhat complex. The reality was grim, and as the enveloping darkness signalled a bitter life in store, Bhoomi, undaunted, marched ahead and sought a space where hope loomed large.

The next morning Bhoomi entered the lanes of a businessman, Gopinath, yet unvisited and unexplored.

An unknown fear has started gripping me nonetheless I will keep my pace faster as I need to accentuate my family income and live life well.

"Bhoomi's work was restricted initially to sweeping and mopping the floors and even looking after the cleanliness of the entire house. Hardly had she known the harshness of her new so-called job. "I wondered why Bhanumati, Gopinath's wife, emphasised a lot more on cleanliness, as the same room needed cleaning four times a day." She came to know that Gopinath's wife was a victim of peculiar ailment. Bhoomi had recently become familiar with terms like 'sanitisation' and 'quarantine,' during corona which had almost become a known term even for the most illiterate. But OCD was a newer term altogether. None knew what it meant but knew that Bhanumati was its victim. Bhoomi was ever more interested to understand but only rested on the idea that a 'Bangali doctor' nearby would best explain.

Unmindful of her mental condition, Bhanumati, Gopinath's wife, continued to torture the servants therein. Bhoomi suffered the gruesome treatment meted out to her. Still, she took courage to withstand the petty harshness of fate.

In every step I give, there is I, me, and myself to give stand
Such thorny ways only double my strength
Pledged to fight the battle of life only to make my grandma grand.

Bhoomi had to bear all the unnecessary ire and the ill-treatment of Bhanumati. Bhoomi believed that understanding other people's psychology would make our lives more manageable. She firmly believed in fate, saying, "With the lapse of one or two days, everything will be in order." Her hopes were dashed when Makhanlal, the gardener who stayed there for twenty five years, said that nothing had changed, the same routine all had to follow. The same monotonous journey had made his life a dead leaf altogether.

In greater desperation seeing Bhanumati arrogant, Bhoomi said to Makhanlal, "Every woman should have the belief that she can make her dream of an ideal society a reality only if she desires. As a mother, Bhanumati should understand that she is the primary socialising agent and the primary factor in developing good attitude of her children. She should realise that equality is not simply a woman's concern but a matter of human rights."

Makhanlal was impressed though, but again thought 'great talks' had no value in that house.

Bhoomi's boldness in pronouncing the words, she could make and remake everyone's life by setting things right fell flat sooner. Makhanlal whispered few words that nothing of a miracle could take place and that he admired her nobleness of character, though.

Bhoomi looked positive and said, "But as for now, let's hope to see the unfolding of a new chapter in a new light."

Makhanlalji was a grief-stricken fellow, and seeing the depression in the whole house, he forgot even to laugh and pronounced that laughter was a rare or rather vanished, phenomenon of that villa. But immediately, Bhoomi replied, "*Babuji*, I came here with a certain amount of hope that my good days are once more on my way and such a woeful comment will add to my tormented soul."

Days rolled, and one day, Gopinath's daughter Anchal came home for a short vacation. She appeared to be a soft-spoken, kind-hearted girl. She slowly tried to speculate everything going on in the house. She called all the outsiders to approach her with their respective problems and ensured the best of her help. She proved to be the one who could give the finest comfort to all. Her words still rang in Bhoomi's ears. It seemed that normalcy was once again restored. But to her utter disappointment, Bhoomi was informed about her short stay and that her plight would resume soon after. The incessant rebukes poured on Bhoomi were almost unendurable.

On her way home, she saw an ice cream cart on that bright, burning afternoon, and her tiny heartbeats again became normal. Bhoomi sensed her resilience. But in a way, she liked this part of the day. But again, she kept her distance as it was beyond her reach.

Watery milk my grandma serves me has so relishing a taste that I can never let it go waste; street ice cream is what I have never chased.

The earth was still drying out, but the sun almost breaking through thick white clouds made it look even more splendid. It was nearly too late, and the realisation that contemplating the beauties of nature would not suffice an inch, she stepped, giving her pace a faster speed thus far unknown.

Shantibai, as usual, was outside her kitchen. Bhoomi habitually gazed at her grandma through the broken window panes. Bhoomi's apprehensions raised seeing the door half opened. She immediately rushed to the room, seeing Shantibai nowhere. Bhoomi's fear knew no bounds. All of a sudden, her grandma came from the back and handed Bhoomi a fifty rupee note. Her silent footsteps were almost unheard.

"Grandma, I am still stunned. This kind of surprise might be the very first instance. Now I laugh aloud; Lady luck to you, I bowed."

Shantibai couldn't hold her smile; her face was inexpressive, so Bhoomi could not gauze the aura.

"I can't bring myself to think about it. Oh, yes, of course, Bhoomi says, remembering it's my birthday."

Shantibai paused a little and asked if she would be partying that night.

Bhoomi replied in the negative, "Unfortunately, no to the utter disillusionment of Shantibai, as the stories of the plight in her new job even disheartened her further."

Grief-stricken Bhoomi could hardly remember her birth date. Unnerved by stories of girl children who were delivered into the other world as soon as they were born.

Such sickening a place this world is that I want to give my birthday celebration a miss.

The untimely maturity of her granddaughter struck Shantibai. Late in the evening, Shantibai tried to ignite Bhoomi's mind as a birthday gift. Bhoomi was sitting cross-legged, holding her ankles for a few seconds, then wrapped herself in a torn blanket. It was a rather cold February night; the room was bleak and brutal except for the lamp, which was quiet and sombre in looks.

A peculiar darkness engulfed me. Is it due to some ignorance? No, I have attained some sort of enlightenment which I need to gift my grandma. They retired to their rather hard bed listening to real-life stories of highways. Scenes of human trafficking involving mainly teenage girls trapped into false promises saddened Bhoomi. Shantibai fed her with her feeble hands a small portion of *kheer* that remained in her memory lane long after her demise.

Bhoomi went back into her world of imagination with thoughts embedded with wisdom.

Our life is a long journey from unknown to known, unfamiliar to familiar, unseen to seen. The quest to learn something new, something still unexplored, remains a basic instinct of a woman. This inquisitiveness sometimes acts as a positive force. It remains a long way in determining the future course of her action. But despite woman's effort to dig up the tunnels of knowledge, she feels pretty helpless in getting an insight into the hidden manifestation of the world mainly because the unsolved arena gets a grand coverage that becomes difficult to break through. Living a life without knowing the end, we are moving without getting a reply to the mysteries, disheartens the caller like an unanswered call. Will it soothe the woman who nurses in her bosom a promise may it be futile or fruitful to unravel and end some part of that unsolved word mystery? Thus, her never-ending Journey begins. The mysteries of the world will be pretty endless. In recent years, the world has witnessed a significant change in the very nature and mind-set of woman, a change not for the good but for the worse, not that she is worse morally or religiously but because she is ceasing to be an individual.

Bhoomi prepared the best return gift she could ever give to her grandma in the form of her marvellous speech. She would keep the wonderful birthday gift from her grandma, which was the photo of 'Lord Krishna', a precious one to be treasured for ever.

Bhoomi's speech beautifully resounded, "A woman feels she is rootless as she is unaware of his authentic self. She is wholly occupied with changes and chances of mere existence. Reality can be those who have attained integration and harmony by overcoming the conflict within themselves. Religion is the excellent remaking of oneself. A woman has to undergo a significant change, an inward change to free herself from the sleeping forces of the enslaved spirit. Religion awakens the real in a woman and recreates the being itself. She is said to be a reborn soul. She sees the divine energy permeating the whole universe. The soul that has received emancipation is free from the bonds binding one to the world."

Shantibai's eyes were almost struck by thinking about Bhoomi's maturity and clear perception of reality. Bhoomi smiled and replied, "Religious discourses in our nearby Sai temple has enhanced my knowledge and fortified me in a way to face life boldly though I break down at times." Shantibai hugged her with a solemn promise never to part ways in the future. It was a fantastic night wherein Shantibai had the best birthday return gift ever to be cherished for times to come.

Dr Sarkar

It was Monday morning, and Bhoomi visited Shiv temple. Lord Shiva is the Hindu God of protection and regeneration. He is one of the three essential gods alongside the creator, Lord Brahma, and the protector, Lord Vishnu. All were offering flower garlands, and the Bhoomi even took the chance to visit, to partake in some part of solace. She collected some flowers, which fell on the ground from the hand of a devotee, believing that a 'sincere heart' is all needed.

I may not have a penny to buy flowers
But I will be rich enough to sell flowers in the coming days.

Such optimism was a noticeable feature of her character. Bhoomi always remained unshaken but inwardly prepared herself for a better tomorrow.

The earth is on the brink of destruction
The turbulent waves of the corona have come with a great obstruction
In the way of human progression
Lord Shiva, we pray you for a peaceful regeneration
And take away all the fear and depression.

Bhoomi believed Lord Shiva would protect the earth provided people won't arouse his wrath. In the innermost core of her heart, she wanted to make Shantibai happier. The little money could hardly make both ends meet. Shantibai but knew that Bhoomi sincerely worked for the betterment of their depilated house. Tears rolled down her eyes, for she could not bear her granddaughter's plight. However, she hardly showed any expression on her face. She concealed it, for Shantibai knew any pampering would only make Bhoomi a weaker creature. Shantibai, in heart of hearts, was all praise for Bhoomi and told her never that she would shine one day.

Late in the evening, Shantibai answered all the queries that Bhoomi had in mind and revealed that the Bangali doctor named Dr Sarkar came to her aid. Shantibai was elated to know about this peculiar ailment and its remedies and instructed Bhoomi on handling a person with this psychological illness.

Shantibai reverted back the words voiced by Dr. Sarkar, "Man has become knowingly or unknowingly a victim of many mental disorders, which sometimes put him in an awkward situation. Others laugh at him, but he goes with it, thinking it is the just action without which his daily routine remains incomplete." OCD, as per Dr Sarkar, was a repetitive and uncontrollable action.

The doctor had given a psychological panacea to Bhoomi as to how to sustain and survive with an impaired mind. He added that even with their desire, these people couldn't control their repetitive actions, as such, Bhanumati's mind had become an repository of some of the most insignificant habits that would accompany her till her death.

Bhoomi was inquisitive about whether Bhanumati could recover as she knew that treatments were available but couldn't give any suggestions to her family as they were reluctant to accept her as mentally ill.

Man in daily walks of life plays variegated roles without being aware of what life is. Life continues, and his activities and behavioural modes, too. Again, pinpointing the loopholes and actions of others has become a part of his daily routine. Thus, life's perspective gets a newer twist with engrossing stories that will take us to a captivating corpus altogether unknown.

Bhoomi thought the religious world would help Bhanumati to recover fast as she firmly believed, "Even the worst of enemy should be loved."

Bhoomi never missed listening to the epic stories of Ramayana and Mahabharata as Janardhan Babu delivered his speeches to give a kind of mental solace to the inmates of the house. Bhoomi once again recollected the day's happenings, starting with the events in the Shiv mandir. Her heart ached to see the suffering of children of her age who were orphans, struggling alone in this virus-fed earth.

When I am down with poverty
I point to the unfortunate ones who have suffered more than me
I think this is the way to feel myself as a blessed one.
Getting a temporary break in this somewhat cursed world.

People crying in agony to see their dear and near ones in pain touched the innocent chords of Bhoomi and said words in a pensive tone, "It was just at the onset of covid, our people need to be extra careful." When Bhoomi decided to work, Shantibai was on alert to put a cover, such as a face mask, which she had made from her torn pieces of *sarees*.

In some part of her belief system, Bhoomi had vehemently reposed firm faith in her prayers. However, as usual, her daily chores beckoned her to continue with reality. She learned that she would be offered double the money for double-time work. She decided to put in extra energy because the little money earlier would not suffice for her grandma. She neglected her inner woes and braved her misfortunes to see the 'little smile' on her grandma's face. But again, as usual, Bhoomi was quite exuberant as the hope of something better was in her mindscape.

Sunny days will be mine
I hope against hope that my days
Henceforth, will be fine.

The following day was beautiful, with sun rays directly penetrating her room. The sunshine seemed brighter as if in a newer attire. Bhoomi dressed up beautifully, and looking at the small mirror, she had a bout of narcissism. She began to sense that she was growing up. She became conscious of her dressing, and twice or thrice, she looked at herself as if admiring her inner self. A kind of 'self-love' had besieged her.

The sun rays have made my face to dazzle brightly
If not anything, the feelings have lessened my pain slightly
Though I know the world has become ghastly.

Again, melancholy thoughts intertwined her mind.

There is none to deliver mercy. Mercy has become a lost word.

"Grandma, had I a place where only mercy exists, we could have lived a blessed life." Shantibai replied positively, "Work is mercy, and mercy is work." Before going out for work, Bhoomi usually sought her grandma's blessings. Shantibai kissed her forehead that day. Bhoomi's joy knew no bound, for she had least expected it. Grandma's usual rebuke got something softer. Again, Bhoomi realized that her grandma was strict with her as she loved her most.

Shantibai's Kind way of delivering words had given her a different look and strengthened her confidence threefold. The heart-melting words had given her a beauty of a different sort.

Grandma has indeed a heart that melts.

The realisation had given Bhoomi a solemn happiness hitherto unknown. Bhoomi's journey had been a few miles, but with a heavy load of experiences, she felt she had already traversed the world. She believed every day would unfold a new chapter, an unknown journey quite unprepared for, yet meeting it with a kind of invincibility.

Nirmali

Poverty is a sure curse
My heart aches to see my fellow friends search
For some money but gets only a grudge
O'God helps all people at large.

Bhoomi was able to voice the sentiments of all poverty-stricken people. She was, in a way, symbolic of what 'ails the poor'. Harsh treatments meted out to Bhoomi because she was a poor lady.

Money is religion, money is god, and sans money, no struggles gained or lost.

Bhoomi could sense a strange kind of silence pervading in the house. Nirmali thronged into the arms of Bhoomi saying, "I want to escape from all worldly sufferings."

Bhoomi gently replied, "Dear friend Nirmali, this world has done too much wrong, nothing in your favor. I understand your plight and will do everything to give you justice, and this is right." Bhoomi's journey through a tiring experience had taught her many a lesson.

The world has two phases, day and night
Day comes after night and night comes after day so do our
plight.

Bhoomi tried her best to understand the inevitability of the situation and that every turning point of life had some solution waiting ahead. She pointed out to the softening nature of human beings and the cruel hardening phase of human nature. Gopinath's wife hardly recognised Bhoomi as a human but as a mechanical machine bound to do her hard chores. She poured all her vengeance and frustrations on Bhoomi by shouting some gruesome words. The softness of the heart, as reflected in Gopinath's nature, only proved the fact that Mother Earth had made this world a balanced abode. At a tender age, Bhoomi grew up having a total sense of acceptance.

The realistic world and the imaginary world are two different zones of existence. God has balanced the fate of every individual. The richer and mightier are happier, which is entirely a wrong proposition.

She thought everyday hard words would no longer be heard as Gopinath was kinder, and a sort of coolness besieged her. Ill fate soon overtook Bhoomi as the least expected chores of watching a neurotic patient became her part. Gopinath's second daughter was an incarnation of the evil goddess. To lie was her forte. To prove her righteous way, she could go to any length. Everyone was aware of the terrible illness, but none spoke a single word. The gardener said that *maji's* days were numbered. Bhoomi remained silent, thinking that *maji* was none other than Gopinath's wife.

She overheard she was the last in the rich man's house to be employed as a maid due to the fear of inside revelation. In this way, tongue-tied girls of the locality, though they knew the heart-breaking dreadful stories, did not utter any word to Bhoomi as the spies moved on a broader circle, fearfully passing every minute. Poverty beckoned her into a world where, unwillingly, one had to accept and resign calmly to one fate. Tears rolled down her eyes, but Bhoomi let them dry in her eyes, thinking that the real world was a much bitter and much more difficult path to tread. She even spoke to herself saying, "I must be different if the world cannot accommodate me. I must be competent enough to face all the eventualities."

Bhoomi had decided to be a better nurse, helping Bhanumati, the businessman's wife, at every step. It was like Bhoomi could not touch food as the rotten smell of stools remained with her. It was 4 p.m., and Bhoomi was not allowed to return home. The terrible day's exhaustion had already fatigued her nerves. By the time she reached home, the lanes were becoming darker than ever.

It could not be darker than what is happening to me.

Such uttering of Bhoomi clearly proved enough, the tremendous mental agony and trauma that she was undergoing; undaunted as usual, she had even the courage to reveal the truth to her grandma.

Again, the gloomy clouds as if signalled Bhoomi for something worse to witness. But hard life had already made her heart a 'hard shell.' Her eyes no longer wept at the pitiful sight, for life's tragedies were what she had been acquainted with from her very childhood.

The happy days seldom shows her face; the little moment soon gets overshadowed by some darker events.

Insensitivity of Humans

The sight of two inscrutable fellows petrified Bhoomi. The whole crowd watched it with the slightest sense of responsibility, trying least to desist the horrifying brawl. Shortly after, a dagger penetrated the young man's belly, leaving him dead. But to her utter bewilderment, Bhoomi saw that none showed any concern, and the whole mob moved away slowly as if 'It's the way of life.' The whole scene visited and revisited Bhoomi, adding a newer facet to her cumulative experiences. The selfishness of humanity had been exemplified in the whole episode, and the dangerous act of murder had paled into insignificance in no time.

The incident has lesser significance for those whose families are not involved, but if we start thinking all as one family, one home, this world will be a better abode.

Alas! It can be realised only in dreams not in reality.
If not own kith and kin nothing touch people's nerves, they only feign.

This realisation taught Bhoomi that the term 'selfless' was no longer in vogue. Her heart gave a clarion call to help that blood-smeared man, but blood flooding the scene gave her a peculiar fear for which she was unprepared. With all its twists, life was sometimes a difficult hypothesis for her. Though she silently witnessed everything that came her way, she hardly fragmented her experiences to know life's proper meaning.

Bhoomi ran away from the sight as fast as she could. She saw nothing on her way, whatever came ahead, just eagerly waiting to embrace her grandma, for she wanted to relate the other unexpected life events. She was oblivious to her daily chores and returned back home. The horrifying news of the murder was in the air, and Shantibai's ears were quite alert to all the latest happenings. But to the utter astonishment of Bhoomi, her grandma showed the most minor reactions, even after knowing about it thoroughly. Bhoomi conjectured that her grandma was like one in the crowd when she replied, "My dear child, the world has taught me all."

Shantibai only wanted to convey the message to her granddaughter that she had matured with experiences and age. Now, at an old age, she was worldly wise. What she expected from Bhoomi was that she should also evolve in the world of reality and grow in the light of truth. That day was an unforgettable episode for Bhoomi as the scene she witnessed would live and relive in her memory lane, reminding her of the reality of human life. Shantibai managed to cook yummy food for her granddaughter. However, she stayed away from eating such delicacies that day, as the heinous scene and the mean mentality of people gave her a bitter taste of this world.

The mental level of humanity has stooped so low
Is there anything more heinous to show?

Bhoomi's face seemed red as if she nursed some inner grudge against those who witnessed the scene. But slowly, it turned pale as she realised, "This is the way of the world. It has its own course which will not change its face, but only mankind can change crooked ways and mean man's face."

Saying this, Bhoomi rushed to her bed; she recapitulated the whole episode with a sense of guilt as if blaming herself for not taking prompt action. Her thoughts were larger than life, something too big to get encompassed within her little self. For Bhoomi, the world means not so big a place, only the area she had traversed and travelled so forth. By weeping inwardly at the helpless condition of humankind, she believed her tears would never go in vain.

Criminals are on the rise no doubt. Uncertainty looms large in our society as crime related activities have assumed dangerous proportions. Its rapid growth can hardly be curbed and is marked by sudden outburst with or without prior warning. Even the onset of a day is marked by bombardment, murder and suicidal acts. Under such circumstances peace getting eclipsed is nothing unusual. The graver part is that man has started showing least concern or I can say, has learnt to live with this lost world.

The conscious being is condemned for his lethargic and callous nature. It is because of this the whole drama of bloodshed gets a chance to re-enact. 'Live and let live' attitude needs a newer outlook with a bit of concern for fellow human beings. At the same time 'human' should rise above individuals and should be determined to take part in the greater responsibilities of life. The aftermath of a caught criminal should be a scene for all to witness and thereby a fear would grip in the minds of all other criminals.

Some page of her life had gone, and Bhoomi had enacted it with maturity, giving it a finer touch, believing, "Our life is full of incidents quite unprepared yet we must accept it because acceptance is another way of living life."

The world has something good in store, and this is not my conjecture but a belief for which I am quite sure.

Questioning and cross-questioning arose in her mind, but for the time being, Bhoomi gave a halt to her constant flow of thought and began to sing some sad, melancholy notes and thus allowed her to pass the time in some way.

Twice or thrice if I delve deep in the happenings of this world, seldom will I get an answer to my call?

The world sans a congenial atmosphere becomes a closet of impossibilities. Tuning into an aura of feasibility becomes some farfetched terms, hardly audible. Even wider vision and higher mission sound alien. In such an improper set up a few lot helplessly stoops to conquer but with a sense of despondency. The journey which stops abruptly is infused with renewed hopes to start anew. Indeed life is a great rebalancing, making mistakes and correcting them always moving ahead towards higher goals and never ever gazing back in anger.

Time as always will go on as it is. One mystery will add to another. As it is not possible for us to solve the greatest mystery,' the mystery of the creation of this universe' which envelopes the smaller mysteries, we can only hope and expect 'time' to be the revealer of all our unanswered queries.

Equality, What an Idea!

Days passed, and Bhoomi noticed that some of the girls were missing from the neighbourhood. She never asked nor sought any explanation from anyone. She also thought like they were doing some hard job elsewhere, but to her utter surprise, she found three of her friends were picked up by a tall man on a truck one by one. But again, Bhoomi did not need to ask about the whereabouts as she thought it might be the call of some hard life once again. The more problematic aspect of life had bound Bhoomi in a way she could not think beyond.

Dear 'suspicion', you can shut up in your castle
Oblivious of my condition, you sometimes become a great
hassle.

One more surprise was on her way. One of three daughters of Gopinath was bestowed with peculiar respect as she had graduated well with distinction.

The love that family members bestowed was, in a way, unnatural for Bhoomi, as girls, according to her knowledge, deserve lesser love than sons. It changed her view that the girl's arena was within a boundary, 'this far and not beyond.' What Bhoomi saw was the happiest site ever, as she thought; she and the girls would have some better luck in the future. Societal change of attitude towards girls would encourage them to do more extraordinary deeds ever known.

Some noble ideas appeared in the minds of Bhoomi's neighbours. People in her locale pronounced that a lady messiah was born to deliver this simple lesson that gender inequality would snap the female folk of all their innate qualities. She was none other than Bhoomi. A girl at an age of sixteen had witnessed the many variegated phases of her life. Life was a great mystery and a rediscovery. She thought that the earlier events passed and the newer events to come would give life a different shape and shade. This grand thought of giving the girls status could even be translated into action by spreading the propaganda of gender equality. Still, again, something kept worrying Bhoomi's mind.

Will my thoughts become great ideas one day?
My belief would indeed come true, I say.

Bhoomi was, as usual, undaunted by any outcome on her way. Life's tragedies had taught her about how to face misfortune. Though the head cook, Shambu, warned that the slightest revelation about the workings of this house or its inner world would endanger her life, she rarely cared as she dared anything on her way. Even she was informed secretly by him that Bhoomi would be jobless henceforth as Vaibhav would take his mother to an ashram in Himachal Pradesh for holistic treatment.

The concealing of a truth will make me ever rude
Soft-spoken words the world doesn't deserve
With only real truth will I serve?

Such boldness clearly indicated that life's pressures could not pressurise Bhoomi to take the wrong way.

She rushed home quickly and reached the veranda, where Bhoomi took a deep breath. All of a sudden, Bhoomi started crying as she felt her hopes were dashed to the ground. Her inconsolable cries could not be stopped, and she finally fell into her grandma's arms, thinking of her as the only solace in this world.

I am shattered as never before by the crooked nature of human being
And the greater hypocrisy, will there be a normalcy and a divine serenity?

Bhoomi's outburst threw Shantibai into desperation, giving her a manifold shock over the shocks she had sustained from her life's misfortunes.

Shantibai echoed the simple words, "Man at times of their life may be in their deepest needs or the hours of estrangement will surely find themselves blessed by the gift of grace."

Seeing her granddaughter mentally broken, she inwardly thought a light teaching would restore Bhoomi to her earlier stricter self. Shantibai spoke in a much composed, self-assured manner which instilled Bhoomi's confidence a lot more.

The simplicity of human beings is a lost word in this world. With the loss of innocence whatsoever, the gruesome reality of this world will never be exposed. The darker sides of humans can no longer be concealed when a part of innocence is still left and is not altogether lost.

The abnormal nature of mankind was the outcome of behaving unjustly to people as in the case of Gopinath's wife as the deteriorating condition of her health is an apt example of justice was never denied in this world. In her lonely hours Bhoomi took her thoughts to be her only abode.

The frenetic pace of the modern ever, disconnected lives has affected the work-life balance. Our daily schedule has been unduly stressed; we must segregate it for the cumulative satisfaction of all. Conscious ignorance is synonymous with lesser interest for life. However, unnecessary procrastination to review the situation might result in something catastrophic.

Shantibai's solemn moralisings had even helped Bhoomi to overcome her mental trauma.

Bhoomi calmly spoke out, "Today's fast-changing world has made it quite challenging to keep pace with it. Instant work with instant results have become the catchword of today's world, where time is seen from a commercial point of view. Even to understand oneself proves to be very time-consuming. This very notion has prevented him or her from understanding the meaning of life. But this does not point to the fact that the one is blind to the reality of life. The person has seen life and passed through all the turmoil but feigns ignorance and even tends to forget that the more one divides one's interests, allegiances, and activities, the less time he or she has for living."

Bhoomi's periphery of mind was well reflected in her words. She thought, "Life's situation becomes easier to handle when one becomes conscious of her natural urge within and that all are on the same footings. Family relations, power, and money are the tools of self-imprisonment from which it is complicated to come out. It makes a man forget the hard reality that we are in death amid life. As we connect ourselves with reality, we find deeper sources."

Our interchange of ideas are enough to make our half fed gut look full
To survive in this world it's the only tool.

It had eventually put Bhoomi to sleep, which was the ultimate refuge for her in deepest agonies.

Occult Science

Early morning, Bhoomi woke up and collected water from the nearby tube well. The well was full of iron, but Bhoomi had little idea about clean water. The formidable task ahead was like a challenge to her. Nothing beyond that she could conceive as days began to take shape in that way. It was as if her taste buds grew insensible to anything.

The rich man's house was not as silent as usual. Voices from all corners signalled that some significant events were in the making. Her inquisitiveness ended sooner as she could see presence of three *tantric babas* clad in red garments and bedecked with human bone ornaments. Bhoomi collected the information that they were invited to treat Bhanumati, Vaibhav's mother.

For all the dynamism and fretting of the present age, the 21 st century man is at odds with himself frantically reaching out for those spiritual moorings which he has lost in the course of his everyday struggle with mundane modern life. Despite the very scientific grounding of modern day society, man now seeks the explanation of his failure and struggles in something super natural, something which cannot be explained by acute reasoning. He feels himself a mere plaything in the hands of those powers and seeks to propitiate them or counter their influence whatever seems more satisfactory. In this world replete with uncertainty a person, in his attempt at overcoming the seemingly insurmountable odds of life in most cases heads to a practitioner of occult sciences. The belief is that through his supernatural powers, the latter would be able to provide major relief to the person in utmost distress.

Again Bhoomi had learned that Gopinath's son Vaibhav was distributing foodstuff to the poor half-fed children as these would throw off evil omen from their lives, as believed. Some religious ceremonies also marked the occasion. The day was off for Bhoomi, but she was there for some inspection to know more about them. Vaibhav believed this kind of act would bestow divine grace. Vaibhav sounded in a somewhat coarser voice that his family was facing a period of turmoil, and he needed some relief on that earthly soil.

Bhoomi was also among those who received a gift from Vaibhav. He hoped against hope that evil days would be eclipsed but believed that divine grace was the ultimate gift to be expected.

Vaibhav said that those poverty-stricken lot had only hunger to fight and once their empty stomach got relief, they had nothing more to shout and were well pleased.

These words fell in the ears of Bhoomi, and instantly, she protested.

Poor have even a voice and an existence which should not be completely neglected.

Bhoomi voiced from behind. Vaibhav hardly paid heed to her voice, but Bhoomi had no regrets as she said, "These futile offerings by rich men will surely go in vain as they do not recognize men as men. They separate humanity based on status, and it is the most hated course they are following wherein no divine grace is inherent."

These outbursts from Bhoomi came as she was wearied of seeing the lifestyle of the rich. The mere hypocrisy and outward showiness were the things she most hated. In the hearts of hearts, Bhoomi nursed a desire in her bosom to wipe out poverty from the world, as it was that aspect that ruined her life.

Bhoomi even thought that one day, she would be the one to be of utmost help to people in need. The little offering would be of a pure heart. It pointed to the fact that Bhoomi was well-cultured. Her helping attitude moulded her into a beautiful girl whose kindness of nature was reflected in her thoughts. She decided to hand over the hundred rupees gift to Prerna, her friend who had frequent asthma attacks. Suddenly, Bhoomi's face glowed as noble thoughts transformed her and her world into a place of divine tranquillity.

I find a kind of serenity in the good deeds
It has a grace in its very seeds.

Though Shantibai was depressed that she could not give joy to her granddaughter, the little act of sacrifice shown by Bhoomi had indeed raised her in her grandma's eyes. Shantibai was convinced that goodness was with her and that Bhoomi was well-trained in the ways of this manipulative world.

An unnatural fear had gripped Bhoomi. She was full of lamentations for the fact that her grandma was in the advanced state of her life. She courageously asked her grandma if the 'fear of death' disturbed her. Answers were full of energy, and Bhoomi ceased to think anything negative. Bhoomi tried to encourage her by saying 'all good' about becoming old.

Bhoomi murmured in her ears, "The art of aging can be a beautiful manifestation of creativity, serenity, and a doing away with how our culture looks at getting older. Over the years, the definition of this inescapable part of our life cycle has gained different status. Some perceive it as a challenge to continue, a stage to surpass their earlier achievements, and even a bitter-sweet attempt to prove themselves to the younger generation. Old age is not associated with depression and loneliness, to name a few. Instead, it shows that older people have better-coping skills to deal with depression than the younger generation. Sociability gives well-knitted protection from the experience of psychological distress and provides a platform for greater wellbeing altogether."

Seeing Bhoomi's abundant knowledge Shantibai questioned her source of knowledge. Bhoomi simply replied, "My *gurumatas* in the Sai temple has taught me enough."

Shantibai always took advantage of every opportunity to teach another lesson, though. She softly said, "Speech embellished with appreciation, goodwill, support, and encouragement can be well expressed with a few selected telling words if only spontaneity, warmth, and sincerity are blended with it. Again she adds few more lines that genuine enthusiasm, interest in the subject, and ceaseless efforts are some of the means that an aspiring speaker should have at his disposal, along with the modern techniques available and accessible to him. Bhoomi added, "A speech can make or mar one's fortunes. So, our thoughts to reach the masses and to be accepted by them simultaneously is challenging. So, even our casual talk should not be cold, superficial, and authoritative. Discussion should always be vibrant with love, friendship, righteousness, and joy. They must inspire the listeners and should not bore and annoy them with ceaseless prattle and meaningless waffles."

Thus, with some hopes and little promises to work for the betterment of society by spreading the right ideas and correct words that became her onus, Bhoomi moved ahead as usual, undeterred by anything worse.

Shantibai really appreciated Bhoomi for aiding her in finishing the lines as her feeble body could not go on preaching for a long time. Bhoomi hugged her grandma tight and cried aloud seeing Shantibai's health deteriorating further. "Grandma I will never let you die." Saying this Bhoomi retired to her bed with silent tears rolling down her eyes in a way that knew no ending.

End of an Era

Shantibai concealed her ailing state from Bhoomi as she could not digest the idea of living alone on this earth. Her fever did not subside for many days, she lost her appetite, and the foodstuffs she most relished became unpalatable. The money Bhoomi had saved was too little for treatment. Still, she braved the circumstances and took out whatever she had in her reserve, for without her grandma, her world would be ever darker. But as ill luck would have shrouded Bhoomi, Shantibai breathed her last before she could be taken to the hospital. Bhoomi was not by her side then as she was busy collecting money.

On her way back home, Bhoomi felt as if something unwanted would happen. Some terrible fear struck her as her intuitions always came true. She was too terrified. She inwardly could feel that Grandma was not well. She was running as she thought she could hear voices of her grandma calling her once, twice, and many times.

The crowd in front of her house made her feel perhaps her grandma was seriously ill. But all her hopes came to nothing as her suspicions came true. It was as if the world came to an abrupt halt. Neighbours failed in their attempt to make Bhoomi cry. One of the neighbours shouted that she was the angel sent from heaven, without whom Bhoomi would have been in the gutter. Nirubai screamed from behind to pick up the body, and that it was time to deliver her to the other world. These words made Bhoomi burst into tears. She remembered how she tried to console her grandma, and now she was inconsolable.

For the first time, she could feel the pangs of utter loneliness. She compromised with reality and mournfully bade her farewell. She braved the inevitable and silently proceeded towards the room of her grandma. The same room with the same window panes echoed and re-echoed the voices of her grandma.

Bhoomi was now dying to hear the rebukes of Shantibai. The villager lifted the deceased body and showered some flowers on her body as a mark of respect. Thus came to an end, the long outstanding life episode.

With tearful eyes, I bid you farewell
Seldom will a day come when you won't be in my mind shell.

It was like a house without a roof for Bhoomi. Her pain was simply unbearable.

I feel a kind of melancholy everywhere. I roamed around the house. I can't settle; I feel as though someone else has been here while I was sitting on the broken sofa. There's nothing out of place, but the house feels different, as though things have been touched, subtly shifted out of place, and as I looked around, I felt as though someone else was here gazing at me. It's dark, and I can hear someone calling my name. Someone calls me again and again. I keep trying to grasp at it...but the further I strive to hold, the further it goes away and is heard no more. Grandma, how I want to be anywhere near you.

The unknown world was a more new and strange place to reside. It was Shantibai who gave Bhoomi an insight into the workings of this world. Her grandma was her pathfinder, the last resort for her. The harsh reality of this world was too much for Bhoomi.

Mankind can sustain pain only to a certain degree
At this age, I have to uphold so much tragedy.

Struggling alone seemed quite an inconceivable idea for Bhoomi as the presence of her grandma was like a shadow, giving her life a secured shade. Stepping into bitter, harsh reality was like fighting the cruel world with painful facts to face, which needed double courage to withstand and sustain.

I must carry the emblem of my grandma to a greater height.

With such ennobling thought, Bhoomi retreated into her real world. She promised to imbibe it with the noblest of ideals and highest wisdom.

The soul levitates to a plane, staring lonely on a lacquered plain
With such a solemn gleaming, no longer to hear good morning and good evening.

It slings away all bars and barriers and needs no carriers
Granny, with whom I have lived with, lurch all of a sudden
into a far perspective
In the loneliest wilderness someday, my heart will cry
For the lovely soul that has been dispersed in the sky.

Kiran

It was 4 o'clock early morning. The calmness that prevailed was never felt earlier. The moment Bhoomi closed her eyes, her grandma appeared before her. The previous night was mysterious in that Bhoomi could hear the sounds of growling, an unfamiliar voice. It simply benumbed her. She relapsed into the world of imagination as if trying to converse with Shantibai. When she woke from her subconscious fit, she realized that her grandma was no longer alive. She felt a kind of vacuum that she had not felt before. The morning was not the same as usual, the sound of birds twittering as if it had not touched the chords of Bhoomi. She could hear whirlwinds of mourning in the air.

The songs of the birds are not the same as usual
Their melancholy is but quite natural.

This pessimistic sense gave the surrounding atmosphere a gloomy outlook. Bhoomi was reluctant to join her daily chores. But the reality was different. Her empty belly was a clarion call to rush to her workplace, as seven days already lapsed. Her inner mental state was evident in her hesitancy to leave her home. Never before was she negligent of her duties.

Kiran, her friend, could well understand her plight. She took the earnest responsibility to deliver the sad news to Vaibhav. Kiran was well imbibed with the lessons from her mother, "The crooked and meanness of this world would not let us live a respectful life."

She tried to soothe Bhoomi in the best possible way, "Realisation and consolation are the best armaments in the worst circumstances." Despite Kiran's efforts, Bhoomi had least reconciled to her lot as the emptiness in her life was too difficult to fill up.

My emptiness is inexplicable
Consoling words are only words
None can take my grandma's place, not even the lords.

Bhoomi felt a kind of emptiness within, that gave her an excruciating pain. Her stillness had snapped her life of all her energy.

Life's course is not at all smooth; tragedy has been what man's lot. The brief seconds fade into insignificance in no time.

Bhoomi's frustrations would not allow her to mingle in the world of laughter. Every new day was a new lesson for Bhoomi as if the day itself was teaching her life's winding tales. Again, nature aided her in giving her solid and mature persona.

Bhoomi pledged never to get disturbed by what was happening around her, both in her life and outside and tried her best to keep pace with reality. Time and again, her grandma's face appeared and reappeared before her, reminding her of the good golden days. Sometimes, even her maturity failed to give her consolation.

A bitter realisation dawned that the past is always past, and living in the past is the most ruinous act of a human being. She decided to leave the past where it was and proceeded with a brave heart toward an unknown future. She believed that life had to go on and none but the 'sole soul' should be its accelerating force to take life forward. Bestowing full faith in her potential, she decided to brave all the untoward, even believing nothing worse could be in her store. She surrendered herself to the altar of God and responded with complete faith in her capacity to face the world.

To you, Lord, I surrender my whole
If none, you are the protector of my soul.

The sense of melancholy was all-pervading. Nevertheless, Bhoomi had decided to protect her sanctity and sanity.

Corona

Heavily burdened with life responsibilities, she could not think beyond her work. A teenage girl would otherwise dream of beautiful things. It was as if the beauty of this world no longer attracted this tiny soul. She thought all good was not her asset and in this abandoning attitude she excluded everything that was imbibed with 'life-giving comfort.' She deliberately decided to join the harsh course of life. She even seemed disinterested in anything that she was not accustomed. Gopinath's house and its daily events were a thing that embittered her life. She decided to discontinue her work because, in her view, none could answer her plight.

Even a harsher work has happiness intact, but work devoid of mental satisfaction loses all its beauty.

Bhoomi joined the municipality's work of cleaning the streets. Kiran reminded her of the scorching heat outside and that it was a terrible blunder she was making.

Kiran also tried to encourage Bhoomi on the other hand and said, "A woman must first realise that she is the creator of life. The thinking process should be reconstituted to consider men and women not separately but simply as two lives on this beautiful planet wherein a woman should consider herself as fit for all types of struggles." Bhoomi gave a soft smile.

I know not which course is better
Though I know my life subsequently won't be bitter.

Life tragedies had not changed her. Her inner charitable qualities had remained, and the belief that 'good will prevail and pervade in this world' made Bhoomi work with sincerity and devotion. The little money from her daily labour was not enough to survive. Still, even she donated something from her earnings to the poorest poor in her *Basti*. Her heart ached to see her fellowmen's condition, but helpless as she was, she never let that feeling rule her life.

I have nothing in my saving
But my soul gets lifted by this selfless giving.
I am the richest, I believe
For I can deliver unto this world everything to give human beings relief.

This worldly-wise saying enhanced her status in Kiran's eyes, who had the presumptuous idea that 'without schooling, none can be educated.' For the first time, a realisation came to Kiran that educated in the ways of the world was much higher than mere formal education.

Bhoomi nursed some sincere belief in her bosom.

Mental satisfaction could only give people a cause to rejoice and stripped of it, all smiles pale into insignificance.

The uneven plane of the ill-constructed road was a hazardous path to tread with. As ill luck would have fallen, Bhoomi was hurt by a pointed rock and bled profusely. It was as if the sight of blood in no way terrified her. Her mind remained firm as a rock, and the piercing of something did not fail to qualify her as a girl of exceptional mental prowess. Standing in the moonlight, the place seemed even more beautiful. With the moon standing as a guide, Bhoomi wondered how beauty could spread in a place full of pain.

The face of the earth has never been so beautiful
It is as if nature's divine grace diffused through everything.

Someone in Bhoomi's place would have lost all the positivism. But not a single voice of rebellion or complaint emanated from her mouth. She had a voice of calm resignation and acceptance. The lack of reaction was due to reasons not far to seek.

Those who live with hope see no withdrawing force ahead.

Kiran gave Bhoomi's smeared leg a bandage and even tried to pacify her broken heart by narrating stories of her plight, even more heart-touching than Bhoomi's life was. But surprisingly, Bhoomi was untouched by these stories as she believed, "Every life has a different story to relate and different significances are attached to it."

Bhoomi tried to explain Kiran about a common woman's crave to do something great. She explained to Kiran in simple terms, "A common woman craves to do something extraordinary. But at the back of them, there is always the feeling that they lack the needed opportunity. But they must remember that all great achievers were not born with great fortune. They have the simple dictum "no pain, no gain" in their mind. But one thing is clear, the sole individual woman's decisive attitude on her part will allow them not to part with their desired path. But the power is within them, and she has to explore it and bring it to the fore."

Kiran was quite astonished to see her friend's view of life. Though she was of her age, Bhoomi's maturity had moulded her into a feminine creature of divine nature.

This is a world where solace and peaceful human living have no real existence. They show their face once in a while as if they are momentarily made to vanish as they appear.

The unhealthy conditions in the neighbourhood had made several people sick. Bhoomi wondered about the unhygienic condition in her local *basti*. Sewage and garbage systems were never correctly handled. The whole *basti* seemed to be filled up with a kind of fear psychosis as deadly corona had taken three of its lives. Life was stunted even from an intellectual point of view. But from a physical point of view, it was abound with inadequacies and insufficiencies.

The menfolk were dare-devil, undaunted by any hazard whatsoever. They decided to carry the sick children to a nearby dispensary. They sought nurses' help in delivering the sick to the world of healing. Their unity was manifested in taking collective responsibility, which taught Bhoomi to render selfless service to humanity. She was pained to see children crying in agony. But their feeble condition was a sight that she brushed aside from her mind as it would weaken her morale strength manifold.

Moreover, she would not be able to withstand the onslaughts of nature. Occasionally, Bhoomi kept reminding herself that 'dangerous man-eater Corona' was omnipresent, much like a demon in her mind. The clothes left behind in her small *kutir* were used by Bhoomi to make masks and wondered, "This is the smallest gift I can give to the people of my dilapidated colony."

Nature has carved me into a strong creature
Misfortunes cannot make me a human of weaker nature.

Saying this, Bhoomi tried to convince her mind that a strong mentality could only help her to exist and that scenes of misery would only lower her faith in God. Her determination to live life from a more powerful standpoint and a hope-filled life lasted forever.

Innocent children dying and mothers crying are scenes that touched my chords.

These scenes revisited her mind, but soon, she had transported herself into the real world, where she needed to stand with courage and fortitude.

I must restrain myself from such sights
As it tends to weaken my inner strength
And the grand battle of life becomes difficult to fight.

Bhoomi was disappointed by life's alleyways, so she walked away from her house, leaving all her memories to be buried therein.

My every day is no new venture
But I can only see misery all around.
Not even a single soul will get spared
Make my life immensely sad.

She slowly crossed a few miles without knowing her future ahead.

How desperately I am struggling to pass my day. I feel my very
breath has been snapped off all its oxygen.

Bhoomi wondered what might be the reason for the Mastermind to keep her alive. Bestowed with a tremendous insecurity, her heart began to beat faster as, for the first time, she felt that she was an orphan not knowing whom to fall back upon.

I still hope God has some Master plan
In sending me out of my land.

Positivism was installed in the very breath of Bhoomi, making her even bolder and giving her the realisation that she had struggled hard for survival in this most insecure world.

Every test was a preparation for her next more difficult test henceforth, as if every day had prepared her to face the world from a more realistic standpoint.

Shivani

Bhoomi's desperation heightened, and simply recalling the earlier shades of protection gave no respite at all—Bhoomi as if had lost all sense of belonging.

Suddenly, she remembered the orphanage centre where her grandma had served, though for a very meagre salary. She never saw Shantibai going to work as her grandma had retired quite early in her life. Her little earnings were from stitching clothes she collected from her neighbourhood. However, with age, Shantibai's impaired eyes did not allow her to continue with the work.

Bhoomi was always desperate to meet Shivani madam, for Shantibai had words of admiration enough for her. Bhoomi took her broken pair of shoes in her hand and decided to walk to the centre, which was not too far. Joys added on seeing Shivani madam for the first time, and her endearing smile was something that Bhoomi tended to remember always. The short introduction was enamoured with words appreciating its owner, Shivani. Bhoomi's adorable words took her aback. Shivani at once invited her to join the centre as a caretaker of kids herein.

Oh! It can be my second home
A sweet place indeed
I need no longer to roam.

Seeing the minors, Bhoomi wondered if her plight was similar to them.

Are we the cursed beings on earth?
Or some more excellent fortune around us lurks
Daydreaming will only keep me stranded in the same place
I need to move ahead to see life's next phase.
Available foodstuffs brought an unexplained joy.
Hunger knows nothing but says never to be coy.

Shortly afterward, Bhoomi saw a jeep full of children. She at once became alert about her duties. Her assigned task was to take the kids to their designated rooms. She even added one more line.

My duty lies in seeing if the kids wear the masks as Covid has made it everyone's need.

A few weeks had lapsed, and one day, Bhoomi suddenly overheard Shivani madam saying some children who were orphaned in corona were kidnapped, sold and that she had well-managed child trafficking gangs all over North India. Bhoomi could not believe her ears as her grandma never missed a day when she would not pronounce a loving word about Shivani madam.

Better if I would not have ears at all.

Bhoomi wondered if ever Shantibai got a scent of what prevailed in this *Anath Ashram*. Shantibai often tried to narrate stories to Bhoomi about child trafficking and how pangs of separation had agonizingly paralyzed children. Bhoomi was sometimes perplexed if her grandma got a hint of something untoward happening in that rather 'heaven on earth' abode. Bhoomi even feared the missing faces might fall prey to the disastrous trade of human trafficking as these gangs had nothing more in mind than making quick money during these covid-19 times. Seeing the kids toiling day and night with physical exploitations around, Bhoomi paused momentarily. A tale of woes was added to her ongoing depressive state.

Is it a suitable retreat?
Or again, life has played a trick.

Speculations apart, she quickly decided to visit Kiran, with whom Bhoomi shared many a life's chapters.

When she saw Kiran, incessant tears flowed as if Bhoomi's life was suddenly filled with horrifying tales. Kiran was quite curious about what had ailed her friend this time. Without wasting time, Bhoomi took her to the nearest police station. The *thaneder* Ramlal listened to the whole episode and even took her photo. Bhoomi got nervous that if Shivani madam got to know, she would harass her innumerably. Bhoomi at once decided not to stop, and both fled from the scene. The least bothered was Bhoomi to see the aftermath of her actions.

I know not about the consequences of my action
I only want to see the kids' liberation."
Two worlds exist in days sunlit
At night, it tends to vanish
The duality of human nature
Is the worst human feature
Shivani is the very devil incarnate
Though I have known it a little late.

A momentary elation engulfed Bhoomi hearing that she was in the news for rescuing a whole lot of children. Bhoomi decided never to return to a rather dramatic world.

Bhoomi even decided never to look back. Seeing mankind in such dare-devil acts made her morose, and an unknown melancholy enveloped her and took her in its grip.

Henceforth, my pace will see no retreat.

Hallucination

Stories of rape, molestation, and acid attack had taken Bhoomi already in the grasp of fear psychosis. She could not keep up the masquerade any longer. She perceived the world full of sinister acts perpetuating evermore.

My self-respect is the greatest possession on earth. I keep it with utmost guard.

Seeing some drunken street boys, Bhoomi became over protective.

Bhoomi jumped into the gutter. Bhoomi tried to hide herself with dry leaves. She submerged herself in that dark place throughout the whole night. In utter desperation, Bhoomi voiced her feelings in words that were inconsolable.

The satanic forces reign everywhere to commit a crime
I want to rest forever in God's shrine.
At this hour, my prayers can act as a miracle
And bring harmony to my desolate life cycle.

She recollected the terrible days and how her fury reached the verge of madness. Seeing her close friend Bholi's agony following a molestation attempt by two boys a fear enveloped her. She painted her feelings in some agonising words.

Suddenly, I find myself lost in a dark alley
I wonder if I lost all my identity
In the far-off distance, my heart throbbing
Seeing monstrous visions
I want to retreat into the world where my granny exists.

Just then, in the morning hours, the medical officers came in a jeep and announced the dangers of the terrible corona virus in very plaintive terms.

"Not too late, Bhoomi gathered courage and shouted at the officers to get back on the right track. Corona is on the way to destroy humanity. "Amazed to see no response, Bhoomi took a slight pause, "Is it my hallucination? "Thus, came a quiet realisation.

To brush aside all the unwanted thoughts of the previous night, she jumped into a pond and cleansed herself deeply. Hunger and frustration had unnerved her.

A boldface can wipe out evil
And makes one Dare-Devil.

From that time onwards, Bhoomi decided to be bold enough to face all the onslaughts of life with courage and keep her 'mental' well-fortified.

A sight caught the attention of Bhoomi; she saw a boy of her age being pampered by her mother. Instead of being sad, she smiled at them and tried to console herself by murmuring some words of wisdom which she thought would suffice her mind and soul.

Maybe their good deed has kept them united. Let all lives be happily lighted.

Bhoomi had some knowledge of the scriptures. She had a firm belief in Karma. Wandering hither and thither, Bhoomi was almost out of breath until it was late evening, and Bhoomi thought of seeking shelter in a temple.

The doors were almost closed, and Bhoomi secretly entered the temple through the windows and hid herself. She vainly spoke to God in words that would invoke pity and love for a girl struggling helplessly for some shelter in this ruthless world.

Beautiful as ever night was
Will it no longer last.

Insecurity was emerging largely at every step. Steeped in reality, Bhoomi kept her eyes open, only wondering what could be the following line of action.

My frantic search for a decent life
Will it remain a dream never to thrive?
Guarding my physical self
Can it be a crime?

Far Away from Homeland

In the deepest corner of my heart, you lie dormant
The inexplicable pangs of pain will never remain a shadowy
moment
Your peakscapes have pulchritude per excellence
Upon me, you have ambrosial affluence.

Bhoomi could always feel the absence of her grandma. However illiterate she was, Bhoomi imbibed the teachings of Shantibai in her heart and preserved it as a precious treasure.

Shantibai always uttered the sayings of Dr. Ambedkar, whom she believed would make Bhoomi a truthful being. She participated in the variegated get-togethers by *Adivasi Shangtha* too.

As a human being, our onus lies not so much in remaking the world but transforming ourselves, thus inculcating goodness in the self and in all humans. Self is the storehouse of immense potentiality, self-alone creates chaos in the cosmos and paves the way for divine peace. We are what our thoughts are made of, we need to refine our thought process and channelise it in a way that would not hamper other's life.

Shantibai believed life has an uncanny way of testing our mental strengths and weaknesses. Such noble lessons had always endeared Shantibai in her neighbourhood.

Bhoomi, silently reposing faith in herself, murmured the words, "My only armament is my wisdom, and that is my only kingdom. We need not make significant commitments to save ourselves but only repeat God's name when we are down with fury or fail; we need the almighty's blessings the most to uplift our true selves."

She rang the temple bells in a way that signalled the mighty paths awaiting her. Thus, taking a silent exit to the roofless world, she stepped miles away from her homeland, welcoming insecurities in undefined ways. She only wondered if life ahead could give her any comfort. Suddenly, rain began to pour incessantly. She took some rest underneath a truck, leaving life to take its course. Bewildered by the insecurity in the outside world and tired by the day's tiresome escapes, Bhoomi could hardly keep her eyes open. She, as if, had yearned for a sleep that would have no end.

My tried eyes need some rest
I want a sleep and no more test
For God's sake, let my mind be oblivious of this world
Sure to wake up at nature's call.

In the deep slumber, Bhoomi was unaware when the truck left that particular junction; to her utter astonishment, she found herself among children in that truck itself.

Girls seemed suffocated as the minors and adults overlapped each other, all frantically searching for a seat. But Bhoomi could see everyone sitting quietly as if some fear had been encircling them; many questions arose, but she decided to observe silently.

I have not a single penny
I know not where this journey will lead
But I have a silent belief something much bigger
And greater is reserved for me.

The scorching heat of summer days was quite unbearable for those girls, but again, they were asked to remain silent. A man with moustache raised fear in Bhoomi's mind, but Pooja, as everyone called, the woman beside them had a calm and composed look which had wiped out all fears initially.

Hunger had almost made her lose all capacities of judgment. Bhoomi relished the two pieces of *chapatis* as simple blessings. Bhoomi pronounced a word of gratitude to the lady, silently uttering words of praise.

You might be one of the Demi-Goddess
For in this cruel, heartless world, there are few
Who can repair loss?

Pooja hardly could remember the faces of girls, and Bhoomi was one among them. Bhoomi's short stature was a boon to her.

Thus, Bhoomi enrolled herself as one of its members. Her future remains undecided, though Pooja had the softest looks ever expected.

I know not what the future holds for me
Where is peace, where is tranquillity?
Where is the ethereal music of life?
Confidence in myself will never fade.
Even in the perils of life I won't be afraid.

Entrap – 1

Bhoomi had a kind of inner consolation promising to face the onslaughts of nature in a bolder way that was earlier unknown.

Bhoomi remained quiet most of the time; her empty belly was ready for any service for a plate of food. Bhoomi placed Pooja on such a high pedestal that she even associated all the goodness with her. Pooja did not expect such an attitude from Bhoomi, a girl of such a tender age. Thinking wisely was her asset; the little meal offered to her daily was like God sent benevolence.

The cries of a hungry man
Is a deplorable sight
A person who offers a helping hand
Imparts a great respite.

Bhoomi stumbled with a feeble voice as days of starvation had made her a weak creature. After an hour or two, they reached their final destination. It took seven long hours to reach *Meerut* with occasional stops. Hiding in sacks of rice, the girls were already exhausted. But as if this frustration and plight were not a matter of concern for Jakir, Pooja's husband, who maintained a detached attitude in ways showing non-participation or disinterestedness. The girls were asked to line up in a way Bhoomi felt suffocated, as the small room was packed with girls.

They were accordingly registered and asked to maintain discipline as the heavy commotion was unbearable for Jakir Ali. He spoke in a typical accent mixed with one or two colloquial English. Ali's harsh, strict ways were never shown the slightest resentment by Bhoomi, and she strictly accepted her fate as her hunger was an answer to all her silence.

I know one thing in this world
People with low incomes have places reserved
I believe for this time, filling
My stomach, my purpose will be served.

Such feelings Bhoomi nursed in her bosom as hunger saw nothing. She left aside all her aspirations. From a very tender age, Bhoomi had learned to face any eventualities, for she believed this mental attribute would help her survive in direst circumstances. But again, she had decided to keep her smile intact even in the most adverse phase of her life.

Every person I conceive to be good
I do not try to see any design beneath their look
This world is a beautiful abode
Gives a balm to lessen man's burdened load.

Bhoomi's positivism was amazing; another person, whether a boy or a girl in such a confusing situation, would try to maintain a peculiar reserve and view everything with suspicion.

I believe mental soundness is the only firm armament to avert and withstand the hazardous path ahead.

With such boldness and a stricter mentality embedded with the grave reality ahead, Bhoomi proceeded carefully with a measured pace. She faced the present without distancing herself from any truth whatever. Pooja's cool and calm disposition was much liked by Bhoomi. From the outset, she was thinking all well about Pooja, hardly knowing anything beyond.

Behind the apparent simplicity
Lies the grave complexity.

Pooja was beset with evil designs as Nargis, one of the girls, cried horrifyingly. Still, it was inconceivable for Bhoomi as she could not think beyond her goodness. Pooja subsequently said she would be their godmother, and queries arising in their minds could be asked without hesitation. The wisest way would be to express all inner doubts without inhibitions that might hamper the unity of the group. Mr Farookh harshly spoke to one and all to adhere to all the protocols mentioned in the wall.

Bhoomi retired to her room and mumbled, "Life has its manifold twists, the present moment will show its list, and the future will never help the present to exist."

Such realisation had elevated her to a higher pedestal. She hid her face behind the masks, silently thinking, "Not following covid protocols is more punishable than Mr. Farookh, assistant of Jakir Ali's hardest dictums."

Such speculations aside, Bhoomi slowly proceeded toward the dining hall.

Starvation knows nothing.

I indeed have to give them something in return.
The girls of my age are apprehensive of their designs
Am I a fool not to worry seeing them not fine?

The morning on that day was unusual as confusion was seen everywhere. It was an unvisited phenomenon for Bhoomi as she rarely witnessed any perturbation herein earlier. She always pictured everything to have a perfect discipline.

The manipulated world and its evil designs are a thing that hardly fall into the arena of my thinking.

Bhoomi had one thing, namely intelligence as her asset. She hardly abandoned it at any cost. But time would reveal the loopholes in her concept of intelligence.

Seeing things from one aspect or one angle is not total intelligence.

Bhoomi imagined the whole group of girls as one family, and seeing anyone missing from the group aroused confusion but never suspicions in her mind.

Surprisingly, she found five of her friends missing. She had the habit of counting all her members again and again. It was funny, though she missed counting herself often. The humour that arose from the miscalculation created unending laughter in the group. Bhoomi now but seriously wondered the whereabouts of her newly made friends. One of them was Farsida, and she was the jolliest among all. She used to crack jokes at every stroke. Her absence created a terrible silence that led to a gloomy aura. Bhoomi, who's positivism knew no bounds, started to view life with suspicion.

The destiny of the poor is always a known factor.

Sitting quietly on the veranda, Bhoomi was trying to recollect some past events of her life, as how the days with her grandma were blessed with a sense of security.

Her bygone days, though more challenging, were filled with reliability. But living in the present as if time had become unfamiliar.

Uncertainty, unpredictability, and unreliability have become
My definition of life
I do not know my future drive
Nevertheless, I will try my best to end my strife.

Immediately after a short time, Bhoomi could hear the sounds of bells ringing outside her corridor. She thought medical officials had come to them to instruct more on covid protocols. She silently made inroads towards the open door and saw, to her utter astonishment, Pooja handing over one of the girls to one tall statured man.

O God! My knowledge seems inadequate to understand reality.

Such desperation voiced by Bhoomi only pointed to the fact that, puzzled by life's web, Bhoomi was at a loss.

Shortly then, Reshma cried aloud as the face of separation from her sister was unbearable, her cries went unanswered. The cause of her agony was a grave realisation that girls were being sold.

Elsewhere, Bhoomi conjectured her newer destinations were unsafe. Again, she had low esteem of her work capacity. She started thinking, "I am an illiterate, I can only be employed to work for Pooja." Time and again, suspicions clouded all her aspirations.

Bhoomi tried to submerge all evil thinkings; the more significant the confusion, the greater her disinterestedness in life would surface. Thus, wrapped with now little hopes, she braved to oust all the untoward events with undefined bravery.

The day outside is an eye-opener for me, someone whispers,
something is going wrong.
Pooja's heart is not that grand and can easily be fathomed
The women folk, I think, are not so generous
As our mother earth.

A Visit to a Zoo

Sitting in the posture of a great thinker, Bhoomi wondered what could be her lot, what more losses had been chartered for her.

But at the same time, she had not left all smiles because she, with utmost hope and without faith withdrawn liked to play the game of fate.

If I perceive the best to happen, something better will come my way.

The next day, Bhoomi was taken with a team to a nearby zoo." I never had the chance to view such an exhilarating scene. Herein, animals have been kept well fed and well protected." Soon, some mixed feelings came to her mind.

The zoo and its animals are as if living

In good co-ordination and seemed to have a harmonious existence,

Are they pleased?
Alas! Had they not been chained
It made me feel my hapless condition and my chase.
How I have been similarly encased.

Bhoomi viewed the zoo with some scepticism. She even began to suspect the intentions of Pooja.

Never before such suspicions have arisen in my mind.

She might bring them to give an impression that they have been similarly captivated. The decision was hurriedly taken without giving the girls time for settlement.

Looking at the Zoo, I feel nothing but languishment
To see life's terrible arrangement
This can never be a lovable refuge
Accepting the high command's verdict is what I cannot refuse.

Sometime later, Pooja whispered in the ears of Bhoomi that she should derive a lesson from the animal world to maintain perfect harmony.

To her surprise, Bhoomi could see tears rolling down her eyes. A dilemma arose as she could see a mercifulness in Pooja's nature. She was trying to release small birds from the cage.

Bhoomi wondered what kind of woman Pooja was, but a belief arose in her mind that Pooja had a heart, if not too big, but had a relatively soft grip. Bhoomi had a momentary happiness that, wherever she still be placed, it's not the worst. The distribution of fruits and foodstuffs to the animals reflected a generous nature of Pooja. This facet of her character brought Pooja to a higher pedestal yet unknown. Thus, came to light some unknown aspect of her nature which was somewhat adorable.

It is easier to pronounce a word against another once we know all their notable traits and character.

Pooja was always accompanied by her husband, Jakir Ali. He maintained a detached attitude, uncompromising outwardly, though. His arrogance, coupled with immaturity, was a thing most intolerable for Bhoomi. Bhoomi silently monitored his steps as he walked restlessly, thinking the trip was a tremendous waste of time and energy. Nothing beyond business captured his mind. Bhoomi pointed out his nature in a nutshell.

His aim of greater business is fixed as an arrow
I wonder how he can be our hero?

Bhoomi rightly pronounced these words as she knew good deeds and human ethics could only make one a 'demi-god.'

Bhoomi's protruding stomach was a callous call to stop all speculations as life had to be lived henceforth. Bhoomi's humour was evident in many episodes.

We the poor are never the cursed ones
Let's wait for our turn
A plate of rice is what we earn.

Instead of becoming inquisitive and trying to prove something Bhoomi decided to move calmly as more negative thoughts would not aid her in surpassing the utter helplessness she had encountered every minute and every second.

Poverty and starvation have at times blocked my wise thinking.

Salma

The days had lapsed, and most girls were deported to their respective places. Bhoomi had made a quiet inspection into the workings of the 'mysterious cell.'

To know about their whereabouts was far to seek.

Graceful designs within the friendly atmosphere were as if dashed to the ground, and the momentary joy was just an illusion. Bhoomi, after that, remained in isolation, believing any closeness with any friends whatsoever would only bring perennial agony. Just then, Salma, a Muslim girl, passed by. Calmly, she approached Bhoomi and narrated the plight of Muslim girls in her locale. She tried to explain to her rather complex terminologies and feelings of religious bigotries that had ruined many. Her long lecture was not at all a subject of interest for Bhoomi, as she retorted, "Religion is difficult for me to comprehend. Its wider canvas has a newer maze; to come out of it is never my craze."

Bhoomi could hardly digest such talks, as these religious topics would only embitter the relationship between the Hindus and Muslims, as she believed firmly, "All religions lead to one god, and the roads may differ; the pathways are beautifully laid with mercy and the fullest blessings from almighty, if only we can perceive it."

Communal violence was spreading in her district, leading to large-scale mass conflicts. Salma's heart ached to see the human mind's ignorance. Her mind could know the cause of humanity's damnation. She was endowed with a typical matureness.

Salma was trying to find a medium through which her voice would get greater expression. She cried out in her relatively coarse voice, seeing the estranged feeling predominating and even wondering if human beings could bring an end to the insensible debate about religion.

Bhoomi was taken aback seeing the reality of voices in their small, suffocated room where they were breathing. 'Good air' for Bhoomi was a bit of solace.

For the first time, I can understand that the human mind can also think great, given a chance, and this reflection on man's mind widened my mental horizon.

Bhoomi realised how human feelings could strike the chords of all, irrespective of age and religion.

This world bitter or better
We have to adhere to its protocol
Having a firm mastery of humankind
Will give us a consolation so called.

Bhoomi could see the depression cropping up in the hearts of Salma. Arising from a sense of realisation of the absolute reality of this world, she voiced the voices of many people who suffered agonising pain due to many problems in the family, in society, and in the religious circle as a whole. Bhoomi, helpless as ever, could not but consoled Salma with few words, "A mature soul should deal with the affairs of the world wisely, time is the solution to all problems, and it's time that is the eye-opener of all the mischievous acts of this world."

Bhoomi reiterated, "Indian society is neither Muslim nor Hindu nor any other but a composite whole where every individual of every community contributes to building the basic infrastructure of our country and can be considered a brick in the foundation of our nation. And if so, we must eradicate from our mind the secret pride that "my religion is truer, and that another is less so. Coming to society, spiritualism and not religious bigotry is the way to sustain peace in matters of religion."

Bhoomi even believed and preached Salma, "People living in a multi-religious society, communal feelings arise inevitably. What is actually religion? Is religion a repository of faith and belief and a way to be a step closer to supreme power or a step forward in showing the superiority of one's religion? It is a sorry state that people tend to forget the real meaning of religion. If achieving the Godhead is the only aim, then why not rise to the spiritual plane instead of remaining within the narrow bounds of religion?"

Bhoomi further added, "Freeing minds from religious chauvinism, prevented all from understanding the real meaning of life. Spiritualism had been stressed because it helped to develop the power of self-control, which remained an essential element of peace. Perfect religious harmony could be established, once the soul gets rebirth. It is the immortal spirit that is lying hidden and manifests itself. It is to realise the totality of the self without losing ego consciousness. A study of all major religions is essential for the understanding of one's own. But no one can indeed master all the scriptures of the world."

Bhoomi's words attracted the perfect attention of Salma and she attached to it some more terms, "The sense of deep spiritual unrest and dissatisfaction will cease if we work for a new spiritual reconciliation and outlook, which should be in the light of recent developments to live together in harmony for times to come."

The passive look was as if given a positive push and was given a chance to rejoice as Eid was in the air. Salma was overjoyed to understand the basic tenets of religion. Bhoomi once again said, "The future itself will pave the way to greater human understanding, only self needs better handling."

Salma narrated how her uncle, who had cared for her, did not finally agree to her marrying a Hindu. Constant physical assault was beyond tolerance; she joined Pooja's heart-to-heart organisation, believing it to be a saviour of all. Still, now she wondered whether her identity would remain such or merge into something newer as poverty-stricken people had nothing to call their own. Bhoomi pointed to her own life as if it were a lesson worth learning.

My future is undecided,
But vision is well-sighted,
Knowledge too is well-lighted.
With such foresight, I remain ignited.

Few more social reality topics Bhoomi discussed with Salma which she had learnt from her grandma. In soft words Bhoomi explained, "In today's world, confusion reigns supreme in people's minds. So long as .the earth remains, various dilemmas will always haunt the minds of woman. Coming to society, one of the vital problems affecting culture is the lack of affinity in people's feelings, possibly due to a lack of closeness between them. The need to interact with people should arise from an inner urge to know about the people and each other's culture. Togetherness, a sense of oneness, closeness, and a sense of similarity is a word of the past in that the relevance of these words has almost become extinct."

Salma deliberately hugged Bhoomi for infusing such positivism with brilliant 'life lessons', which she thought was impossible with the ignorant. Salma even narrated to her the significance of Eid of how Muslims enthusiastically welcome the holy Eid and embraced each other wholeheartedly and also how they gather at one place, 'Eidgah,' to offer holy prayers of Eid. Salma even explained to Bhoomi how Muslims offer Zakat, Sadqa–e–Fitr to those who are underprivileged and thereby get showered by the grace of Almighty God, Allah. Salma softly said, "This Eid belongs to all; no wonder one is rich or poor. Donations during this festive occasion ensures the survival of the poor and bestows ample happiness amongst all."

Salma promised to be her best friend forever, and Bhoomi reassured her of every help in the most alarming situations of her life.

Deception

Late in the evening, Bhoomi had a chance meeting with another 'distressed soul.' It was as if she was not given the lesson to laugh. Bhoomi noticed from the very outset that whenever all laughed, she hardly slowed any interest.

Bhoomi conjectured if the disinterestedness was because miscellaneous apathies had surrounded her.

She was Anju, a girl for whom crying aloud was her usual forte. Bhoomi's despair was evident in her words.

The poor have no place in this world
My house is, in reality, the open street
I curse my fate, realising it, I will never be late.

Bhoomi pondered for a while, "I can understand her heart-wrenching mental agony, and now I am almost breathless, seeing no ways from any angle as how to help her. So much belief these girls had put on Pooja, hope God our final protector would guide her thought process in a way that might not hamper anyone's interest."

However, Bhoomi lived at the mercy of Pooja, she could also act as a consoler and counsellor of many, seeing sadness around and only thanked her grandma for giving her worldly wisdom as how to remain pacified in the untoward circumstances of life.

Bhoomi rightly said the words, "The girls have no definite guide to revive their disturbed souls."

Bhoomi decided not to hear any other life stories of her friends as she believed, helplessness forced all to become the same and become a part of the same destiny. Just then, when Bhoomi was in her thoughtful loitering, she could hear Pooja, her ultimate caretaker, screaming aloud.

A sudden feeling dawned in my mind; my time of separation has come, but no wonder I have an undefined sense of calm resignation. For the imaginary world was most short-lived and hardly could be the abode of any earthly dwellers.

It was an unknown destination, though, and a fearsome thing for a seventeen year old girl, but Bhoomi was unnerved and undaunted by that final call from Pooja. When asked to dress in newer clothing, which she had just brought from *tailor master*, she waited patiently to hear from Pooja the whereabouts of their next tour.

Though inaccurate, it was a short trip to one of her lost brothers.

Reasons unknown but I am delighted to hear that separation is not in my cards right now. But I have inwardly prepared my mind for any eventualities.

Bhoomi noticed the foodstuffs that were given could no longer captivate the attention of her inmates. Bhoomi remained silent as ever and cleverly watched all the movements of Pooja, for she believed wisdom without intelligence is worthless. When Bhoomi spoke of the intelligent factor, it was clear enough to mean the winning of good over evil.

Any crooked application could only foretell evil, I am pretty confident to thwart off any devil.

It was the house of Nawaz Ali. Bhoomi hardly knew the exact location of the new place, which was a sight most unfamiliar.

I smell something fishy.

From a tender age, Bhoomi was searching for the truth behind the scenes, and this nature persisted. Even when left alone, she faced the world, and this particular aspect stood her in good stead in the most turbulent periods of her life. Bhoomi was reluctant to accept the drink from the Nawaz. She could perceive some apparent link between them, hidden from her knowledge. Bhoomi's frustration grew as the duality of human nature was what Bhoomi detested.

On one hand, she was sympathetic enough to shed tears even at the chained condition of animals.

I wonder whether it is an act or a deception.

The manipulation of this world was a thing much hated by her. Circumstances encircling her were so puzzling that she could not hold her tongue without saying something about life.

This life's labyrinth and its wild chase has been the experience of one and all.
Anyone who negates this cannot be called man in the truest sense of the term.

I overhear Pooja saying to Nawaz, that some promises would be accomplished by her a week later. Still, for the time being, some delivery plans are being made to harness her proceedings desirably.

Bhoomi silently thought and rethought what might be the business of Pooja. She heard stories from her grandma about how girls were sold to Kabuliwalas and how they were lost forever. But again, leaving aside her negative thoughts, Bhoomi thought of Pooja as a caretaker, a godmother she believed could not do anything sinful.

Thinking's of man has no endings; it is impossible to know the working of an individual mind; the greater one intrudes, the greater the loser he becomes.

Thus, Bhoomi very cleverly defined the boundaries of the human canvas. And without digging deep any further, she decided to take each day in an adventurous way.

Uncanny Dream

Bhoomi now decided to follow the life's destined course with a curious mind. Roofs of security had been shaken for Bhoomi for the second time. Nevertheless, believing that dilemma is an unending factor of the human mind, Bhoomi began to think the solution as an inconceivable idea. Bhoomi debated within her mind, the vexed problems facing humanity and whether any one hand came out victorious.

Tranquillity is a lost term whenever I am put to a stern test.

Fear of being caught had caused Pooja to change the location of Subeda and Muskan, permanently somewhere far from their lane.

I am yet to outwit Pooja. Pangs of separation from my bosom friend Muskan make me look horrible. Transporting them to other places makes me more terrible.

Muskan was of her age, she was brought here with high allurement, namely a factory job. Taking Subeda as a confidante, Pooja had disclosed the malevolent trade to her, that that house was a destination for sexual enticement and nothing sort of human enhancement. Many times, Subeda tried to inform the local police, not when Subeda could see police as a part of this malicious business. At this time, Bhoomi became more conscious of herself than any thoughtless wandering. Bhoomi could smell something unwanted and 'that all is not well'.

The hypocrisy of human existence has remained a riddle for generations. This small yet significant episode of double separation will give me a hardened maturity.

The world stage had taught Bhoomi enough.

Camouflaging, lying is only the trodden part of the people.

Bhoomi delved deep into an introspective journey, "My hazardous path is laid down with thorns. It is purely at my discretion to decide which way is desirable, whether to bleed or give a tight bandage to my wounds silently."

Bhoomi was also aware of the futility of devoting time over issues that would take decades to bring about its downfall. Instead of losing her mind to diverse angles, she submerged herself in her self-belief system with a sense of righteous justice. Her melancholy in times of embittered circumstance is evident when she said, "My birth is questionable, so insignificant a creature that nothing remains answerable. "

The night was as chill as her feelings. A kind of unusual coldness overshadowed Bhoomi's usual warmness.

The revealing of life's facts brought into her mind a sort of depressive overview.

The meanness of humankind, accompanied by embittered feelings, had visited me many times and made me mentally weak. I tried to close my eyes, but every time Salma appeared, the fact that I can give a sigh of relief to Salma gave me hundreds of consolation in my heart. Can I aid some more in terrible mental distress?

Bhoomi never expected praise from the outside world as she had lost all her hopes. Bhoomi treated praise as an unnecessary appendix whose existence is baseless. She believed, "If one is genuine and knows their action to be in its proper place then any praise or embellishment cannot lift them further.

Suddenly, Bhoomi fell into a deep sleep. With the onset of morning, she related to Sharmila the fearful nature of last night's dream. Salma was seen as if calling Bhoomi to relieve her of her mental agony for the second time. Salma was as if trying to say something, but voices were not as distinct as many times Salma appeared and vanished. Bhoomi had the intuition that all is not right for Salma. Even Sharmila interpreted the dream as a bad omen.

May be evil days surround my ways.

But Bhoomi could not comprehend how dreams dreamt about others could be hers. But without such debate, she nodded and said, "Maybe my evil days do not want to leave me like others." But the fact that all was not well for Salma came to her mind repeatedly.

One of the workers, Qadir, called Bhoomi to help him in the kitchen. She remembered quick service was the primary rule that needed to be followed. Bhoomi at once stood up but accidentally got hurt as broken glass pierced her feet, and she bled profusely. Bhoomi exclaimed in agony, "Oh God! My leg is stained with blood." Sharmila gave a bandage, torn from her clothes to make her stop bleeding as if it provided consolation to her already ached torn heart.

Bhoomi would not allow her soul to be touched by any stains as it was the only possession remaining within her controlled domain.

The greater the pain in my life, the greater the enduring capacity I have gathered.

Bhoomi decided however grave life's miseries might be; she would remain unmoved.

The slightest weakening would only lessen my life's strength to face the most challenging test of nature.

Bhoomi was wondering what could be her life later on. The whirlwind events that encircled her life till now was part of her forlorn destiny.

I have to act my enacted role in my short phase of living.
Why does so much confusion persist i wonder?

Bhoomi passed the whole day in a confusing turmoil and said, "To move hither or thither, so heavy a mind loaded with variegated responsibilities, I wonder if I am an old lady or a teenage girl."

Bhoomi very often passed comments that evoked humour. She sometimes laughed a lot that remained a noticeable feature of her nature. She believed, "The self can make or mar happiness, we are the creator of unlimited fun or dismay. Can we not laugh or play?"

Even who has nothing but stays merrily in life's worst state of affairs is a richer person.

Bhoomi's views on life defined her mental state and how she kept it smilingly protective. She wanted to share the wisdom she accumulated from her grandma with her friends.

I am able to sublimate the heat waves of Salma and that is the kind of success I have achieved in handling mankind.

Though Bhoomi was little abreast of the girls she met and the friends she made, she only prayed that they might be 'safe' in some secured places.

Drug Racket

The night fell as never so sooner, and Bhoomi, as if deaf to all the sounds, looked towards the streets where she was standing.

I see the stars twinkling from afar
As if telling me to become a lord's avatar

She used to watch two men quarrelling, the typical scene every night, and after a few pauses, talked to each other, sharing food too. Just then, she could hear clouds bursting. Bhoomi derived consolation that she had a roof above her. The rainy days might be horrible for them, she even wondered.

A noticeable feature about them is that one used to be away at night for at least one hour. The other used to watch the scene in a very nervous manner. She used to monitor the scenes, to pass the time casually.

At night, even time used to pass very slowly. The men in the street looked rather shabby with a thick blanket wrapped around each one. That night was unusual. Bhoomi decided to study the scene rather seriously. After an hour, the other man returned and had a short conversation. She decided to watch every moment with the coolest determination to watch the exciting episode again, wanting to unearth something. Suddenly, one of them wrote a note on the pillar. At 2:30 a.m., a man stepped out of his car and took a screenshot of the message on the post. After the car left, they suddenly woke up as if sleeping was a pretence.

Bhoomi had the habit of gazing at the streets for hours from her little balcony, at night which also kept her awake and alert. She finally decided to dig the whole incident as curiosity got the better of her. A woman with an amiable disposition smiled at Bhoomi daily during morning hours without giving it a miss. Bhoomi took the help of her friend Nitu, who knew little about reading and writing. The entire incident was written in a piece of paper and thrown downwards into that woman's lap. This time, Bhoomi raised her hands in the manner of something that she wanted to convey to the lady beneath. The inquisitive woman quickly picked up the paper and took an exit. Days rolled on, and the lady became inaccessible.

A week later, Bhoomi learned that a vast drugs mafia chain was disrupted, all due to the efforts of an unnamed girl. Five police personnel were arrested in connection with the drugs menace case bearing one kg of Illicit drugs worth approximately one crore in the international drugs market, and drugs seized too.

My identity is hidden though
I am happy none can escape my vision.

Bhoomi could feel a kind of divine happiness. She thanked her grandma for giving her a solid infrastructure with fullest intelligence.

I need to recreate myself by reinventing my own rules, and all my actions must be natural and executed with the finest ability.

Terrifying facts came out that these two men were smugglers supplying drugs to the local youths. It was a respite to the hundreds of mothers and wives almost on the verge of panicking.

Actions, great or small, don't matter; achieving some reformation will bring peace in the days later.

The drugs control administration had unearthed and busted a spurious drug racket and largely succeeded in making the place drugs-free. Thus, one small yet significant drugs network had been cracked down with Bhoomi's aid.

Pooja repeatedly asked Bhoomi if she was the mastermind in busting the drug racket. Bhoomi remained in her natural posture without giving her a hint of her active part in the entire racket. She maintained an absolute silence and feigned total ignorance.

Momentary exultation gained through baseless argument is only a pyrrhic victory.

Events after events added to her chapters of life. The feeling of exhilaration would no longer persist for long.

Pooja, her godmother, had heard about these acts of bravery; though outwardly she praised an unknown girl, in the heart of hearts, some fear had encircled Pooja, as the girl in the newspaper resembled Bhoomi a lot more.

Pooja felt her trade would be exposed sooner and soon decided to deport Bhoomi to a newer destination but soon changed her mind. Bhoomi chose to take a sympathetic disguise only to escape fate's brutal hands.

Safety an Alien Word

Bhoomi dared to see the aftermath of her stays with her so called godmother Pooja. Her dare-devil attitude towards life had infused enough courage. Bhoomi decided to train her willpower so that she might not step back in reforming society. Soon, a much-unexpected thing happened. She learned the inside story of Pooja from the slave trader Zamal Khan. Bhoomi exclaimed, "Safe is hardly applicable in this insecured world." Bhoomi expressed her frustration in words inexplicable.

Oh God, have I been oblivious of the realities of my otherwise secured world of Pooja, I would have been much happily placed. Pooja's husband has been deporting girls to Gulf countries, earning huge revenue. Pooja's money transaction deal is hardly known to any of my friends except the couple themselves.

Bhoomi overheard the secret conversation while passing through the main hall, and even the earnest appeal by Pooja to stop this deadly trade was given a deaf ear by her husband. Her cries were unheard and request made to her husband not to trade with the girls was turned a deaf ear. Adamant as he was, he hardly paid heed to any of her appeals, as Jakir Ali had only business in his mind. A cursory glance would reveal their darker side underneath. One thing evident from the entire episode was that Pooja was a better human. Bhoomi was so terrified witnessing the entire scene that she exclaimed in utter agony, "O God, can doomsday be even worse than this."

The hypocrisy of this world was too much for Bhoomi. Her mind started to swing between two poles, "To become a spy or to maintain a detached attitude, what could be the better route?" She carefully knitted out the plan and realised, "Keeping pace with this world is the best choice whatsoever."

Bhoomi believed complying with the request of an evil-doer is the greatest sin ever. Pooja's thoughts did not tally with her husband's mind, but her partaking in her husband's evil mind pushed her to the list of the devil. This categorisation came from a simple heart who had previously thought humanity was not so demeaning. Bhoomi was maddened by the fact that she had placed such optimistic hopes in this world.

Am I a fool in judging the so called world so incorrectly? I have no pathfinder; even God has withdrawn my support. My earlier positivism gets a severe blow. How can we expect something great when the meanness of this world is very much prevalent?

The sense of belonging seemed to get uprooted. Bhoomi suddenly took the image of 'Lord Krishna', and started chanting prayers to save humans from all evil clutches and devil's designs. She remembered the 'Krishna Janmasthami' celebrations in her locality which was held with utmost devotion. Krishna is the eighth avatar of Lord Vishnu, the protector of universe. Shantibai never missed to take her to Vishnu temples on Janmasthami. Her singing of the slokas of Bhagwad Gita still rang in Bhoomi's ears.

I can remember some of the sayings of Lord Krishna in Bhagwad Gita." For him who has conquered the mind, the mind is the best of friends; but for one who has failed to do so, his very mind will be the greatest enemy."

Bhoomi henceforth decided to guard her mind vigorously.

A Bet with Anupriya

The everyday world of Bhoomi became an existential one; for now and then, Bhoomi was thrown aback into such a situation that her very reason to live got a tremendous tremor. However, she did survive the attack or assault of fate or whatever might be termed as life. Bhoomi had the greatest asset of having possessed an intelligent brain. She would quickly adapt herself to unwanted elements in an undesirable environment. Her ungrudging and humble nature were all the lofty ideals she was crowned with.

Only an abnormal act will convince them that I am no longer a threat to Pooja.

Bhoomi decided to sort out her plan in a careful manner. Acting was a thing in which Bhoomi had a special kind of expertise.

Once Bhoomi could recollect how she cried for an hour, none could convince or console her. Bhoomi played a bet with her friend Anupriya, who repeatedly told her that Bhoomi was the most hated object for her grandma. Seeing countless tears rolling down her eyes, Shantibai even began to weep and mumbled words that could not console her. In no seconds, Bhoomi's tears were dried up.

The joy and merriment were restored once and for all. Shantibai was doubly confused and could not understand the whole story. Bhoomi immediately replied, "I want to confirm my grandma's love for me." In such cases, Bhoomi excelled even with her superiors and friends in befooling acts.

Bhoomi once again tried to restore her earlier acting calibre within herself. However, this time there was none to appreciate her acting endeavour. She had to satisfy herself and prove to herself only.

The slight deviation from my role in acting would endanger my master plan.

What was demanded from Bhoomi was careful precaution. She ousted from her mind that she was enacting a role only to save herself from this double chained world. Bhoomi always tried to prepare her part in acting, to be very normal without the smell of acting therein.

The spontaneity shall not be disrupted by any other thoughts no matter what comes ahead.

For a time, Bhoomi thought, "I have to resign myself to my fate."

Soon, the anger arose of what can be termed a peculiar kind.

For no fault of mine such grave injustice has perpetuated my whole soul. I will break the bars, break the whole story to the world.

Soon, the realisation dawned that such hasty actions would lead nowhere. She would be lost in that unnamed world as any other insignificant creature. So, the wisely formulated plan, though it may take a little time to translate into action, would be a greater solution to her heart-breaking problem. She decided to bring all her intelligence to the fore.

With such heroism and a firm repository of faith, Bhoomi proceeded with her plan, taking her acting skills as her main armour against the onslaught of this rather vexed world. Sometimes, Bhoomi even wondered if she had really become insane. As she believed, "One cannot be normal in this abnormal world."

Circumstances till now had transformed Bhoomi into a being stripped of all its life support. In this terrible mental distress, she sought final consolation from her very mind itself.

To act the part of a lunatic person will be the easiest for me as the days ahead will surely make me a terrible mad person.

Pooja's trade was a hide-and-seek game; the false assurances and huge margin of hope shown would never be excused as the curses of many helpless girls would surely work.

To believe that we poor girls have no reason to smile, have no reason to live at our own will is a huge fallacy.

In her helpless condition, Bhoomi visualised many similarly chained girls struggling to escape captivity. She questioned the fact that people experiencing poverty had lost all their claims. So for the first time, Bhoomi cried aloud. She thought her poverty was a great curse and felt that despite her prayers, she got no relief from any corner.

Totally broken a girl, how can I emerge from my present lot or am I destined Oh, Lord!
Again to win over our loss is the greatest victory ever.

Bhoomi rehearsed her part several times in a day, some comic events she tried to recollect to make her life situations easier as many times she said.

My life, or anyone's life, is a chapter already written; we only need to be fine actors. Man's life is surrounded by a succession of divergent problems that are inevitably encountered and must be coped in some way......Nothing can undo what has already been done, but man at least has a chance to remake the future and make the world better.

He should also realise what it meant to be a human being, and that man had a significant contribution to make, and the very act of understanding and acknowledging his or her potentialities might constitute an advance over what has gone before.

Pooja, The Showstopper

Pooja grew suspicious of Bhoomi as days passed by. She felt her trade would be finally exposed if utmost precautions were not maintained. She thought of keeping a watch on the movements of Bhoomi. A kind of trepidation encircled Pooja. The next day was a visit to a place that was not revealed earlier. As Pooja was quite unwell, Bhoomi was asked to accompany her. Again, on the other hand, Bhoomi grew suspicious of Pooja's evil designs.

I remain calm. I have decided not to be too docile or hostile but to maintain a balanced posture.

Suddenly, Bhoomi saw hosts of boys and girls dressed as beggars. Everyone was well-trained in their respective roles. Pooja was still for a moment as the much-unexpected things happened. The children made entry through a different route. She could not control her anger at the same time; it was challenging to throw dust at someone's eyes. Pooja was tensed, but Bhoomi was unable to gauze. The whole situation needed to be understood.

The comic part is that I thought it to be some theatre party
So many child artists at one time to see is like a dream come
true.

Just then, Bhoomi could hear the sounds of drums beating aloud. It was 7 p.m. She was so excited to see the whole team that she rushed into the room with others. There was a terrible thunderstorm that evening, too. Bhoomi took advantage of the darkening situations around them. In that dark, Bhoomi was hardly noticed by Premlal, the caretaker of the so-called beggars. There was thunder in his voice, grudging everyone for not meeting the standards. He warned them, that he would disband them and thus would leave them on the streets forever if they did not follow his orders. In the meantime, Pooja was in search of Bhoomi. Searching in every nook and corner proved futile. At last, she was found sitting near the exit door.

When asked why she was not found in the hall, she feigned ignorance about the whole situation and replied, "I have fallen into a cosy sleep as my tired eyes need some rest. I think it a better place to close my eyes."

Pooja breathed the air of relaxation for the second time, thinking that luck had been in her favor that day lest the joint trade would have been exposed. She nervously asked if Bhoomi knew these boys and girls.

Bhoomi simply answered, "Not the same as we are; they are mere actors playing their part as we act our enacted roles on this earth." Pooja now thought that her pre-supposition that Bhoomi's intelligence could outwit all was a false presumption as their trade of employing boys and girls as beggars could hardly come to the notice of Bhoomi. But the reality was that a darker phase of Pooja came to light.

I tend to pretend that nothing is happening, though I have come to know of the dirty trade that Pooja is pursuing.
It is like showing disrespect to real beggars.

People could now hardly distinguish between the real and the faked ones.

The gruesome reality of this world is too difficult to see, simultaneously, I believe all the facts have made me mature in the real worldly sense of the term.

Such outbursts from Bhoomi clearly pointed to the fact that the world as the best teacher and guide had made her more educated, giving her an insight into the workings of this world.

Pooja decided immediately to release Bhoomi from the locked bars and allowed her to move freely inside the whole building. Her promises were enough to infuse a belief in Pooja. Notwithstanding her terrible mental sufferings resulting from the ghastly deeds of Pooja, she confirmed her mind to remain numbed as staying that way would only help her save herself from the so-called malevolent situation.

If we live with our doubts, our life will even betray us as our acts become contemptible.

After being asked to move and mix freely, Bhoomi needed clarification about which part to tread with and which would be more secure for her. But for the time being, she decided to maintain coolness and thus pretended as foolish. That would be her other part of acting, as Bhoomi believed. "I hope I have not become a spy agent and master detective." Bhoomi even sometimes thought about the futility of her actions and plans.

World is much harsher, and every path is laden with a maze; all depends on the ways we devise to come out of this great trap.

All these comments pointed to the fact that a girl who had so much hope in this world had lost some of her positivism, which was so strong with her earlier.

The next destination is quite unsure, and the next event is relatively unknown; never before every moment offered something so new that may be expected or most unexpected.

It seemed a pathetic condition for Bhoomi, her reason to live was put on hold.

A Peep into a Den

The heavy promises of Pooja did not convince Bhoomi. She thought every move of Pooja had some motive behind it as she also imitated the very footsteps of her husband.

Bhoomi decided to watch every movement of Pooja this time to unearth another hidden story. On the other hand, Pooja couldn't convince her mind that Bhoomi was still the innocent child of nature. She doubted her intentions as again multiple questions posed by Bhoomi only enhanced her suspicions further. Putting aside all this never-ending inquisitiveness, Pooja reclined on a sofa as if she wanted to have a short knap. Sometimes, Pooja was so frustrated dealing with this kind of ignoble trade that she wanted to embrace death smilingly.

Bhoomi sat on the veranda the whole night as the loneliness enveloped her in a way she had never known.

Death is the only way to deliver to the place of eternal gracefulness. But even death has been ruthless to me as seeing me in pain and thereby prolonging my life, my pain has been increased manifold.

Speaking to herself loudly, Bhoomi felt some justice had been done. She told Hina, her fellow mate, how challenging it was to live in a world of manipulations as it infused our every breath with more suspicions. Hina even related her story of how she was married off at an early age and the turbulent situation she had to face after the demise of her husband. Hina was a bit older than Bhoomi. Still, she had a torn heart and believed the world had not yet started any institution of justice.

Bhoomi tried to give her the most consolation by simply saying, "If we believe something good is happening, then indeed good will pervade and prevail. Whoever has nothing in life, has but hope to make them stand firm and erect amid circular agonies everywhere."

Bhoomi believed, "Every human being is a storehouse of wisdom and that great lessons in life can be learned from everyone.

Bhoomi's thought process clearly implied that she wanted to accomplish some extraordinary and something praiseworthy.

Our life is nothing but enactment of a drama full of stories of agonies and frustration and a titbit of satisfaction here and there. Self-destruction results from human criminality so outrageous that even the highest art cannot do justice to it. At some point, the man feels threatened by the meaninglessness and the absurdity of life. Nevertheless, he goes on. Man can decide his future and make our mar his fortune. He should feel that he has a responsibility to the whole of humanity and not merely to his adherents.

The natural reason of man seems at first to shine brilliantly. Still, it is, in fact, a torch in a misty night while the inner light of proper reasoning seems to burn perennially and shall grow up from a fair hope. A modest assurance, that light shall never go out not the works of darkness, not the prince of darkness ever prevail upon us.

Bhoomi explained to Hina some core facts of life. She said, "Youths are on the threshold of a new destructive spirit. They live on the plane of ideas rather than of reason. Girls entering the business of bargaining their bodies may be for economic or other reasons, but why? Mental satisfaction should be higher than monetary success."

Hina even cried how she had stepped into the wrong world. She tried to find out if she had any information about the reality of Pooja. Several men and women coming and going were scenes to witness from the corridor therein. Bhoomi was about to burst out, but her maturity had taught her to listen more and not to speak out abruptly. But surprisingly, in the afternoons, Bhoomi could see Hina talking with Pooja in a manner that couldn't convince her eyes. Bhoomi was stunned as she believed Hina's story to be true. Bhoomi said in a shivering voice as if she couldn't come to terms with reality.

My world is again shattered.

Even farfetched dreams could not give solace to the otherwise little Bhoomi. At one time, it was such that she used to build her hopes and aspirations on plans, assuming it was the only home for those who could not realise things in reality. Bhoomi used to think again and again, all that was possible was only in a dream world. Surprisingly, Bhoomi once confessed to her grandma, "Things which I think and think for a long time get materialised in real life."

Shantibai gave a sweet smile as a reply to all her queries and said that reality was so immediate and urgent that she hardly had time to think beyond.

Bhoomi found these two worlds entirely devastated, so fractured was her view of life that she found herself completely lost. Her very definition of life started changing from that point of view; abandoned by two worlds, she could not define her identity as ever. Bhoomi even wondered if she had any identity ever attached to her, "I decided not to speak a word of complaint or resentment as the least outburst would endanger my life." Bhoomi agreed not to talk a word of criticism or irritation as the least outburst would threaten her life further. With such intelligent course of action, she thought she would not be viewed with suspicion as Bhoomi believed, "Life's satisfaction depends not so much on trying to prove another right as to oneself as right." She found some contentment and said "I am satisfied that at least

God has made me aware of the grave fact, if not at the first stroke but slowly and slowly."

Twice or thrice I have thought
The pros and cons of my angry outburst
But it will result in nothing
Other than the loss of an intelligent mind."

From the very outset, Bhoomi kept her wisdom and intelligence as the only armour that needed to be preserved and well-formulated, as at most times and throughout her journey it was the only resource available.

Hina

The same evening Hina once again approached Bhoomi in her usual white attire. Her face seemed terribly broken. Bhoomi hardly paid any heed to her relatively coarse voice but, yes, gazed at her continuously. Hina just then whispered in her friend's ears if anything ailed her. Bhoomi remained indifferent as she could not completely recover from her panic-stricken state, "I am saddened by seeing the ultimate acting of Hina and that remaining silence is the only panacea left."

On the other hand, Hina started suspecting Bhoomi whether her 'make-over' had been discovered.

Further silence will only make everyone around curious.

Just then, Pooja entered their room to overhear the conversation between them. Bhoomi wondered why Pooja had to spy on them; maybe she had lost faith in people like she had lost her say in everything around her. Though outwardly she poised herself as a powerful lady, inwardly she stood powerless as visible in her decision-making cases. Pooja played some tricks to wipe out the suspicions lurking around in the minds of Bhoomi. It was Saturday evening, and beggars usually lined up in cue near the temple with the hope of getting some *prasad.* Pooja took some used clothes and packed them up in a bag. She saw the bags fully loaded with clothes. Bhoomi wondered what might be the next possible plan of Pooja.

To study the mind-set of humankind is the hardest task ever.

Bhoomi was tired at the very dubious ways of this world, but still decided to monitor the movements of Pooja within the four walls of the house chamber and beyond. Unable to get any scent of her consequent action, Bhoomi became more inquisitive. Pooja had distributed whatever black clothes she had in her possession to the unfed girls and boys.

Surprisingly I can see some burkhas among those clothes. I wonder and ceaselessly ponder on this issue trying to explore its variegated possibilities. Perhaps her team of actors needed them to further beguile their cruel hearts within.

I got stunned for the second time when I saw seven of them are my roommates. I can see a greater game within that game now. I am now determined not to support Pooja and her cause any further. My innocent self has been drowned in the ocean of many mischievous acts. I believe aiding an evil mind is an act hardly pardonable.

Pooja's winking at the disguised beggars as if hinting something, was a scene Bhoomi hated to see any further. Bhoomi now decided fleeing from that scene was the only possible means left. It was not an easy task as some spy group monitored Bhoomi as per some information gathered. Seeing Bhoomi so distracted, Pooja got curious and asked the possible reasons for keeping a faded look. Bhoomi replied in a rather sickening way, "My energy level has stooped so low that my body and mind have been sapped of all its vitality. I need some rest madam."

Pooja was even more surprised when she addressed her as madam, as normally she used to call Pooja. Pooja could realise that something was seriously wrong with Bhoomi. Bhoomi's eyes flooded with curiosity all the time, only pointing to the fact that she was not in her earlier self, watching all unwanted movements in this grave world.

Oh lord, take my breath away to an unknown destination as I am perpetually tormented and know not how long my virginity will get protected.

Entrap – 2

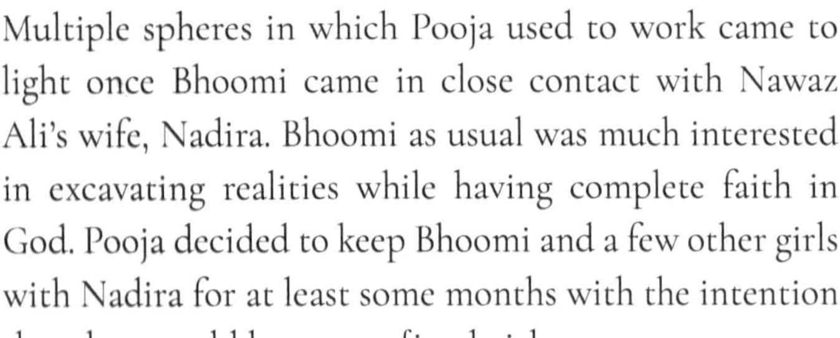

Multiple spheres in which Pooja used to work came to light once Bhoomi came in close contact with Nawaz Ali's wife, Nadira. Bhoomi as usual was much interested in excavating realities while having complete faith in God. Pooja decided to keep Bhoomi and a few other girls with Nadira for at least some months with the intention that they would become refined girls.

The training program included teaching eating etiquette and developing a sense of stylistic living. Basics of spoken English was also included in the program to bring these girls to the level of a civilized lot. Pooja lovingly said to Bhoomi that nothing untoward would happen with her. Only that she wanted to see her as a perfect child of nature groomed with the best of qualities. Bhoomi replied, "Pooja, you are always for my well-being and in improving my life's pathways I shall never doubt your noble purpose."

It was like an escape for Bhoomi from the monotonous journey travelled so forth. Bhoomi even decided to shift to her newer destination with abundant hopes infused in it. Just at the moment when Bhoomi was ready to get dressed up, Pooja stopped her.

I wondered about the possible reason for this abrupt call to wait; I am asked to dress up as a Muslim woman, all fully covered except my little eyes through which I can view the world.

Bhoomi could now understand the whole story behind the distribution of *burkhas* to the sitting beggars. Nadira's project was well set up. Her programs included educating girls and making them the perfect girl for her trade.

Nadira was a woman of a typical type. Though she was a perfect idol to her husband, her acts are set apart from the rest. She believed amongst heavy malevolent acts pervading the premises, she was at least doing something noble. Nadira was God-fearing and believed that only good deeds would transport her to the beautiful heaven still unknown. Sakira who was under Nadira's guidance said that a middle-aged woman though, Nadira behaved like a small child, sometimes too innocent, that she turned out all, not letting anyone to kill a fly.

At the outset, Bhoomi feared that even her religion had to be changed as a first step before getting inducted into that school of refinement. Bhoomi pleaded with Nadira, "Let me remain as me only."

Nadira could feel the agony underneath a girl in the vortex of fear, whether for fear of changing religion or anything within that corpus.

"My tears are like drying within myself; I even forgot what tears are meant to me, whether made to console or overflow the tragic phase of life."

Nadira just smiled at Bhoomi. She was confused about whether it was meant to give some consolation or a sarcastic smile, smiling at the never-ending predicament of a pitiful soul.

All the girls newly inducted were given an introductory lecture about the rules and regulations to be maintained. Days rolled into months and newer episodes only added to Bhoomi's anxiety.

I feel myself to be in grave captivity, somewhere I feel a kind of solace that Nadira, though not superhuman but still a lady with integrity of character and values, and attached to it is her nobility of purpose.

For unknown reasons, Nadira always tried to keep Bhoomi in safe custody, protecting her from all odds even trying to save her from evil eyes. Bhoomi was even surprised how the whereabouts of many of her inmates got lost in the vale of oblivion.

"I am still safe, perhaps I have done something good in my earlier life. Now, as a young girl, I could feel how my thorny life is but studded with flowers of success as my virginity is still well protected."

Bhoomi hardly knew that many a trade was carried on with her by making her unconscious again many times.

Sakira questioned whether Bhoomi's success meant only the protection of virginity. Bhoomi smiled and nodded as if anything could happen in an unknown place. Sakira could not digest her idea of success as her success meant only money and nothing else. Bhoomi once replied that the definition of success varied from present to present. Sakira asked Bhoomi if she knew the brutal secrets of this three-story building. She explained to Bhoomi about 'Date-Rape Drugs' used to seduce a woman out here. Sakira said that on consuming it, the opponent becomes powerless to give a self defense, largely confused and unable to recollect the earlier events later on.

Sakira firmly believed no living organism escaped sexual assault in this theatrical abode. She expected a sort of pandemonium to arise, but Bhoomi remained calm and composed even after hearing the most terrifying facts getting exposed. She simply replied, "I resign myself to fate."

I believe in ultimate destiny
It will make me one day free
From this dark dungeon which I only wish to abandon.

An Inescapable Dungeon

Nadira was born and brought up in a good family. She was initially a Hindu Brahmin, but love had forced her to embrace a different religion. The painstaking labour she had undertaken to learn and unlearn was a significant phase of her life. Bhoomi was told to understand terms like 'love Jihad' wherein love knows no religion and where no societal pressures can stop a Hindu woman from marrying a Muslim. Bhoomi showed least interest in such topics.

I do not attach any significance to these man-made terms as they have variegated interpretations.

But Nadira told Bhoomi as a forewarning that the house where she lived was a base of pain and pleasure. Abundant sacrifice could only lead to future happiness.

For Nadira, life entered a different stage when she embraced Islam, that she had been separated from her parents and bereft of love from her dear ones; one could easily gauze her plight. Bhoomi's resemblance with her sister gave Nadira enough consolation to her otherwise dead soul.

Bhoomi replied in a low voice," I am honoured, madam."

Seeing Nadira so close, Bhoomi felt free enough to express and give an expression to her inquisitive mind and said, "Dear Nadira, I miss my former caretaker, Pooja, a lot more. She had never called me once she left me in your closet." Nadira then conveyed the sad news of how Pooja committed suicide a week after she kept Bhoomi in her custody.

Pooja's mind was encompassed by guilt as event after event she was harassed mentally by her husband and his entire family. Nadira recollected the last words Pooja told her over the phone but which she could not reveal to anyone. Pooja expressed her utter frustration," Nothing can be more inhumane than flesh trade."

The last call perhaps warned Nadira that humans could not escape the ultimate penalty if wrong had been done to any living man or woman. Mr. Jakir Ali, Pooja's husband had asked her to send all the girls to Sonagachi in Kolkata, for unknown reasons. Nadira said to Bhoomi how helpless she was as Pooja had been removed from her real mission of giving the girls a means of livelihood. But no aid from any corner; she had taken the last resort that was accessible. Nadira tried to explain Bhoomi featuring Pooja as a virtuous lady ennobled with lofty ideals.

Bhoomi cried aloud, saying, "I am orphaned again." Nadira at once took her in her bosom, consoling her in a manner promising much love hereafter.

Pooja had instructed Nadira to take special care of Bhoomi. Her truthful and bold nature had already set her apart, so Bhoomi thought it might be her final destination. Still, Nadira once said no place could be permanent as nothing definite could be predicted in this world.

Bhoomi agreed with Nadira that they were moving towards a world where uncertainty could only be seen. Bhoomi expressed satisfaction with how Nadira handled her and saved her from evil clutches. Nadira's firm friendship with Pooja had helped her to keep her promises intact. But again, she hinted at how putting different disguises on Bhoomi had, in a way, helped her to achieve her ultimate goal. Nadira knew trade, knew no emotion, and life was more brutal ahead, so one should handle all with precaution.

Suddenly, Bhoomi started begging Nadira to release her from these bondages. She wanted to get released in the truest sense of the term.

No more captivity, only freedom will give my distressed soul a pristine look.

All her hopes were suddenly dashed to ground as Nadira simply said 'no'. It was as if a terrible lightning had struck her, making her standstill. Bhoomi was as if unable to pronounce a single word, something seemed holding her throat tightly. Shortly afterwards, Bhoomi returned to every day thinking that her repeated pleas were useless.

Nadira tried to convince Bhoomi that the norms were such that anyone staying here had either to stay forever or had to be despatched to some unknown land, from where one would never come back.

Intoxicants

Bhoomi realised that her life had to end in this dungeon only, and this made Bhoomi worn out beyond measure. Now she decided that her life was made either to die by suicidal act or to flee without hesitating to break all rules in the process. Serious revelations, one was that steroid injection, oradexon which caused fatal health hazards was prevalent here.

A thought came to Bhoomi, "Dying is the easiest route for an escapist. Though I have had enough pain, I was born not for abandoning my life but to live a life." Even in the direst hours of her life, Bhoomi vowed to take a courageous stand and never to look back in anger. Bhoomi could relate to a childhood experience when she fell from a mango tree while trying to pluck mangoes. When asked about the intensity of her wound, Bhoomi smilingly replied, "My will is in my domain, well protected. How I can be wounded..." Such was her reply that Shantibai was taken aback by her alarming maturity. That was her conception of pain.

Just then, Nawaz Ali ordered all officials to operate only at night. Nadira interrupted his decision, and her many manipulations somehow made his plan go wrong. Nadira was determined to execute her dream project in her own way. She would foil all interferences at the first attempt. Bhoomi silently braved life's multiple challenges. *Changing one's appearance at another's will is something I scorn.*

Bhoomi never protested, as protestation would result in nothing. Her voice would emerge and submerge in the same flow, hardly allowing it to transcend beyond this enclave. Bhoomi's frustrations were imminent, but as if there was none to pacify her pitiful state.

I believe hurting one's will and conscience is much more sinful than anything. Again, passively accepting something without protesting also lies in the series of greater sins.

Bhoomi seemed to have lost all faith in Nadira, thinking, "No further relief can be expected living here. I must find a chance to escape as only damnation, no salvation is written on the walls of the so called prison."

Bhoomi's survey too, suggested that none had escaped.

I must change history.

Unable to decide where to start, she planned to remain quiet as ever, as silent plans were most fruitful. Bhoomi felt some suffocation as liberty was not in her cards. She quietly pondered on her life's course and how she had to traverse the unexpected and never wanted to rest; such was her attitude toward life.

Nadira gave Bhoomi the ultimate hope that the day she would be released, she would get a higher pedestal. Bhoomi also thought her little education would give her a higher position. Bhoomi overheard the conversation going on in the main hall. She could hear lots of commotion and was perturbed, thinking what could be the reason. Bhoomi heard saying 'fixed rates on different girls.' She could not understand the real implications but thought it might be a serious discussion. Later, she learned that the better educated would be sold at higher rates. Hearing this, Bhoomi was disturbed beyond the extent so much that she chalked out a plan to befool the world. Nadira had put on variegated makeovers, even forcing Bhoomi to wear *burkhas*, which Bhoomi most disliked. Still, she decided to use it for her benefit. She quickly dressed in her old patterned attire, as the *burkhas* are the most fitted ones in such a turbulent situation. Bhoomi, as if forgetting to cry, started laughing at herself.

Do I ever expect this journey?

Bhoomi now decided to be very realistic, abandoning all her futile imagination as she needed to shape her life map better.

Mishap

Bhoomi every time threw herself into the thoughts that could breed no relief to her. Reclining on a bed, she thought life had no rest and a minute passed was only a preparation for the next immediate venture. The evening turned into night, and Bhoomi started to think about Nadira. Though forty five years old, Nadira thought herself too young a girl and asked everyone to address her by her name just like Pooja. Slowly afterwards Bhoomi decided to come back to reality as to her, real world had to be accepted in some way or the other.

Bhoomi could hear the sounds of horns ringing aloud, as if asking the batch of girls to get ready faster. The night was as chill as her fear. She heard footsteps.

I tried to record those voices and monitor those steps.

A few hours later, two of her so called friends informed Nadira that the mini bus that had carried the girls met with an accident, and many succumbed to their injuries, the driver was drunken, and the mini bus passed straight into the river just fifteen minutes after the start of their journey. Bhoomi humbly prayed to God, "You have safely delivered them unto the safe world, those were the blessed souls."

Bhoomi, as if envied them, their death was a kind of relief to the otherwise cursed life on earth. Hearing the news, Nadira ran as fast as she could to the main hall, shouting aloud to the top of her voice to send men to rescue them and to send everyone to save those girls as they were freezing in this cold night. Nawaz Ali's desperation was imminent as he incurred substantial monetary losses.

The night was as if a curse. We had to wait until dawn.

Nadira was vehement in her protest. She feared until the following day, only dead bodies would float.

Living with those girls I have built a peculiar bond with them; I can still remember those girls bidding me farewell.

Nadira gave their etiquettes a fine polish. They never forgot to wish Nadira in a little bit of English coupled with Urdu, which ennobled them further.

Bhoomi wondered if they had known the real intention of Nadira, they would have hated her. But the overall situation was very depressing as they were also human beings with plentiful aspirations. Bhoomi said this as she could understand the man's cry in distress. A thought came to her suddenly as it was an excellent chance to escape.

If this chance gets missed, my life will remain imprisoned forever.

Bhoomi wasted no time and was on her exit way in no second. The whole aura was gloomy, notwithstanding what was happening, Bhoomi carefully planned her future action.

I must run otherwise time will run away.

Bhoomi's decision was wise in that, chance gone was gone forever. With careful precision, Bhoomi drew the exit route map in her mind. The small gate through the underground tunnel remained locked. Bhoomi followed the footsteps of Anya, Bhoomi's friend and finally unveiled the secret exit door. One slice of it always remained open. Very carefully, Bhoomi hid in the wooden box underneath. The moment the guard left, Bhoomi escaped through the tiny window panes, and finally Bhoomi breathed the open air. Initially, she couldn't inhale oxygen properly as freedom remained an almost alien term for her.

These days and months in captivity has made me forget the air outside.

Not resting, she hurried up her steps as the fear of being caught made her almost nervous. Bhoomi would miss her friends, but this time, she had fortified her mind that no emotions could make her weak and unstable. She heaved a sigh of relief.

To be in captivity is hell, on earth, we need to be free.

Bhoomi, amidst utter desperation, never ceased to think that life had infinite possibilities and immense potentialities in store. Various twists had already made her visualize life's worst phases. Still, once again, she was free in the world of infinity.

I will not be cheated anymore.

Such bursting out indicated that people born and raised in slums are bolder and more determined than ever.

By some bouts of ill luck, Bhoomi was caught by the guards of the 'house no 33' where Bhoomi stayed.

Nothing could be worse than what is happening to me.

Soon, she regained consciousness, and to her surprise, she was again in the same room from where she had escaped.

Unnecessary delay has caused my present state to fall into a trap of misery again. Many a life battle I lost in questionings and cross questionings; sadly, stepping into reality, I have to be one among the desperate souls again...

House No. 33

The passing phase of life was not just an unforgotten episode for Bhoomi. Every path trod was laid with many unseen misfortunes.

Sometimes, little positivism and later that too got overshadowed by untoward unexpected things, and that had what exactly diminished the brightness in Bhoomi's face. Nadira's house was like a horrific prison.

'House no 33' had one exit gate wherein a mysterious script was inscribed on the outer sign board as an excellent grooming house cum hostel where food and accommodation were free. What went inside was never meant to be known by the so-called outside world. Nadira sent some girls residing in that most fabulous hostel to newer homes, never to return. The pangs of separation were too heavy a thing to bear again. False id proof making was a daily scene to witness.

Bhoomi was almost tired seeing multiple actings in Nadira's house. She told Sima, one of the house cook, how she almost escaped the evil clutches, "But guards picked me up, maybe huge awards awaited my catcher. I feel now that I have been more chained than ever."

Bhoomi decided to work on her plans instead of sorrowful mourning. Just then, Bhoomi stumbled and fell on the muddy ground; her mud-smeared hand became similar to the dirt inserted by this dirty world into her body. Bhoomi could hear a voice whispering in her ears, "Always think that you are the undisputed ruler of yourself."

Bhoomi no longer cared as to what the aftermath of the incidents would lead to. At one time, she felt sorry for all the friends she had lost in that fateful accident. But again, Bhoomi decided to work on her successive plan, believing she would emerge triumphant. She took the same exit route a month later, collecting all the inhalers that could make a man unconscious. Steeped in an arduous task, Bhoomi nevertheless remained fearless. Bhoomi remained ever indebted to Anya for helping her to escape from Nadira's enclave.

I bid adieu to this world of mafias and traffickers
I need to rescue all from these human attackers
Sadly, leaving my friends back
Hope I am on the right track.

Seeking Almighty's help, I advanced towards the same exit road map. This time, success is mine as several rehearsals have made me competent enough to escape unheard and uncaught.

A week passed, and Bhoomi collected titbits of food from charity houses. She could still remember Shantibai saying words that could invoke in her abundant confidence to live life with courage. Bhoomi, from a very tender age, hardly complained about her fate. She had the habit of counting success. The mere failures could not demean her spirits as she is the possessor of an abundant winning attitude which gave her a victory over all minor hindrances.

Even encircled by turbulent waves of depression, she kept a smile, getting geared up for a newer and free destination ahead.

I do not want to mention the hazards of how I spent sleepless nights to anyone as there is none to offer me consolation.

Bhoomi was mature enough to handle life with care and live independently. She believed that if we viewed others lives, all life would tell the same story.

Life needs no pacification and explanation as man has to endure and get themselves cured.

Gay Rights

Bhoomi, a girl at a tender age had become worldly-wise, she believed in the dictum that change was the only reality, the right mind-set and the power of positive thinking were a much-needed arsenal or tools for a better life. Educating one's outlook towards a better end would amplify and enlighten multifarious minds. Living in harmony with one's will would only be beneficial if rightly directed. Bhoomi, for whom the betterment of the world remained her motto for existence, for whom limitations, personal liabilities, and excuses were imperfections in worldly terms, nursed abundant positivism without any cynicism whatsoever.

Bhoomi saw a huge procession with protestors carrying placards, 'Gay rights need protection'. Bhoomi couldn't comprehend the exact meaning, though she had learned little English.

It's just a passing phase of life, though I cannot digest the whole idea.

Boys falling in love with boys and again marrying persons of the same sex, can ever this idea be conceivable?

Bhoomi was quite curious to know what it really signified. She eagerly approached a man in a black hat who seemed aggressive. He stared at Bhoomi, which was neither in a manner of flattering nor a threatening one. He looked genuinely confused.

If his eyes seemed angry or objectifying, I might better know how to show reaction; instead, he seemed mild and pleasant but surprised.

In no time, the man got deeply engrossed in the procession.

My views had no significance amidst the hues and cries of many elite protestors. It is not for general mass but for a section of people for whom the world has become a mess.

Though Bhoomi had no formal education, she believed she was equally eligible like others to pass comments on ways of life. The so-called black cap man expressed that 'gay right' equally applied to all Indians. Bhoomi found the talks and situations very awkward.

Forcefully imposed ideas have no permanence.

Bhoomi uttered some words imbibed with the highest wisdom, "Only time and no human beings can be a great educator, and only time will decide who can be acceptable or unacceptable."

Bhoomi was well-versed in the art of camouflaging. Dressed in a man's attire, Bhoomi moved confidently in the rally.

To have my stomach filled up does not necessarily mean that my ears also need to be filled up by things which seemed weird and absurd to me.

At times, she had to struggle with the reality that her education remained undone and that it might hinder her knowing and understanding life process. She passed by the same man again, only to hear the most boring lecture ever. He repeatedly told Bhoomi about the need to understand life deeper and that 'freedom of action would get the fullest expression only if she realised and understood life's 'craze and maze'.

Bhoomi could not easily digest these perplexing concepts, and at best, she decided to remain silent. Coming out the faithless world of captivity is like a phase most craved after. Dressed as a male, Bhoomi could feel much more comfortable, though sometimes confusing too. The unknown world, its unknown people, and strange events marked her everyday life. Leaving the man in the lurch, she quickly took an escape route only to inhale the pure air and that unwanted talks would not chase her anymore. A few miles ahead, Bhoomi saw a few people staging a hunger strike across the street. Bhoomi did not want to explore reasons whatever. A few minutes passed, and Bhoomi could visualise a more incredible drama behind them. They were relishing foodstuffs at the back of the curtain. Bhoomi was shocked beyond imagination and only wondered if life had anything good to offer other than the dubious acts of humanity.

The world is unfurling its hypocrisy in its fullest terms. I cannot become a silent spectator to these gruesome facts.

The canvas of life was much more comprehensive, and life had much more to unfold. Until then, she tried to redesign her mind-set positively, thus trying to embrace life in all its facets.

Bhoomi's quick escapes did not point to the fact that she was an escapist.

I am tired of the ridiculous ways of life.

Nadira's spiritual master had also trained Bhoomi, only to realise whether she had taught her to be spiritually enlightened or some other missions hidden underneath.

So many venomous acts and worldly follies have I seen that hardly a day has passed when my day is at peace.

I, Bhoomi finally decides to forget all earthly woes as days, weeks, and months of tiresome phases and unexpected turns and twists of life has made me overburdened.

Bhoomi had some security, but the false disguise and great make-up couldn't give her real happiness as when she was in her authentic self. A silent realisation dawned,

"Women, however strong, cannot be physically strong compared to men."

Tensions brimmed full in cases of women, especially when security issues are concerned. But at the same time, hiding one's real identity would not be an enduring and lasting idea. Again, however good an acting was, once discovered with just a mere flaw, could ultimately lead one traced to his or her roots.

January 2022

I have some long miles to go and must travel carefully lest my treasured hopes will get tarnished evermore.

Retreating into the past would hardly give Bhoomi some kind of solace, as the bygone days would never relive again. So, extracting imaginative happiness was the thing most futile. But at least one point was clear, Bhoomi needed no more acting and disguises.

The old days with grandma was, in a sense, golden, etched with the fullest security. Those carefree days are a thing of the past.

Sometimes, Bhoomi even yearned to move to her native place, but at times, a thought came to her, "Returning to a place with no dear and near ones would hardly soothe me and my lost soul."

The forgotten routes, once the most trodden, had not left any imprint there, and Bhoomi wondered whether her *Basti* ever mourned her absence. Again, some positivity could be seen lurking around her, as evident from the words that flowed from her mouth.

I have voiced my voices against many social evils and distributed homemade masks to my greater family. They must have remembered me, my silent prayers, that they remain alive still.

It was the first of January 2022, the waves of coronavirus surged in the first few weeks, but the death rate was relatively low. Bhoomi's eyes soared as fear of the death of some of her long-lost friends surfaced in her mind. Overlooking the past grief and a positive belief had given her life a great push. Bhoomi always tried to attach meaning to life, even though it might not be how she deserved it.

God has some master plan. When the rich and poor alike are afflicted with it (deadly coronavirus), isn't it a reminder that humans are one and same, with the same physiology?

Time and again some thoughts kept disturbing Bhoomi.

The only way to get united with the people of my basti is to return there.
I need to remember my once most trodden route.

Bhoomi was restless to return as the fond memories of her forgotten bye-lanes haunted her the most at this time. The variegated test she had to pass within such a short period was like a nightmare.

I see myself living in an alien world
As Raghu now, I feel my soul is two-fold.

Living as a boy, Bhoomi now tried to view life from an altogether different angle. Bhoomi thought, "Nadira's long lecture on gender equality was but a fake picture of reality." For now, she wiped out all fears from her mind. *The mob in general may discover me.*

Bhoomi could even remember Pooja saying that girls are on par with boys. Bhoomi could now negate what she said and proudly proclaimed, "Boys are much more at ease with their life, and their 'will' remains undisputed."

The man's will is universally unchallenged, only to realise later that girls can be ever more superior to male folk. All rested on the thinking process. Bhoomi tried to recollect her grandma's 'New year' words fondly......

The onset of a new year is the beckoning call for something new, abandoning older subdued feelings of hatred and animosity and encompassing within its fold a somewhat lost terminology called oneness.' In terms of a mass movement towards greater human goodness, more incredible human excellence, and greater human understanding, it is the only way to create many revolutionary ideas to set the chaos in the cosmos right.

The human mind has become a vacuum, giving every unwanted element a free pass. Rediscovering within oneself a power to realise one's potentiality and the ability to visualise and realize one's dreams will give life a 'reason to live. But the strenuous effort seems to go in vain when one sees the outside world beset with deadly terror. The trauma of living a life full of insecurity and restlessness instead of rekindling one's spirit dampens it to an unknown extent.

But again, as it is said, sometimes a breakdown can be the beginning of a kind of breakthrough, a way of living in advance through a trauma that prepares you for a future of radical transformation. The wave of newness is like a reinvigorating tonic that will make one oblivious of everything that was wanted or unwanted and will prepare us to oust the bleak present for a better future...

A month later, Bhoomi felt sick; a kind of uneasiness swept her as if her whole physique had undergone an abrupt disruption. The fever rose, and it hardly showed signs of subsiding. She rushed to a nearby hospital, and much to her relief, regular paracetamol tablets rescued her from death's captivity. Her feeble health was a thing Dr. Manju was a little too worried.

My regular check-up is done.
Corona vaccine is in my bold blood now.

Bhoomi realised how delay in taking a coronavirus vaccine would have almost killed her. A harsh realisation awaited as Bhoomi could now reconnect to what her friend Sima had said that, Pooja had died of corona and never a suicidal act.

Pranaviram, the head pharmacist, took the utmost care of Bhoomi and revived her to a plane of almost entire recovery.

Disguised as a boy will only enhance my security; how about Dr. Manju, who looks after human race safety. I must throw the false masks aside and dress myself in a girl's attire. I know I have been already discovered by the one and all in this hospital.

Her meeting with Pranaviram was a turning point in her life as love began to open its petals beautifully, ushering in a period of love. But again, Bhoomi had decided to subside her feelings for the time being.

Without pondering too deeply or considering the pros and cons of her actions, Bhoomi moved ahead. She could not decide whether it was infatuation or genuine love for Pranaviram.

Bhoomi wanted to come back to real self to restart life anew.

Not happy with God's creation
Will only demean me as a human being
Let's honour the creator's divine plan
Let me reconcile to my lot and relive life on my real self.
I am the reborn Bhoomi with a newer soul
Sans knowing my ultimate goal.

Love Blossoms

Living without knowing the end towards which one is moving or without getting a reply to the mysteries, hardly would alleviate the soul who nurses in her bosom the desire to unravel that mystery of life. To be overwhelmed with love, awe, and admiration, we need to feel something absorbing something that grips us and connects us to the strange and powerful ways amidst the surreal surroundings. The mode of our action even tends to become more and more irresistible and try to bind us more within its clutch.

Love blossomed as never before. Bhoomi felt a kind of tingling in her fingers, and she felt at times breathless.

Oh! This is not corona
This is the flowering of a new fondness
A voiceless language trying to bring the dead to life
Is no excellent magic signalling love to thrive?
I need some clarification about understanding.
He is in a newer version of my confusion
We are gifted with so huge a sense
Our love is of most entire magnificence.

Bhoomi confessed once, that life's turbulences had made her forget about anything that is love. She was again not sure if it was the feeling of infatuation or real love. Pranaviram hardly spoke a word of confession, a soft-spoken person who spoke more with his eyes. Bhoomi was exuberant to find a person who had helped her enough. She tossed herself gracefully into the arms of Pranaviram, hardly knowing the consequence of her action. Lady luck favoured her; when he spoke the one line that he was starting to have feelings for Bhoomi.

Pranaviram smiled at the ceiling. Bhoomi paused and started looking at the blacktop, worried if it was the expression of his love for her. He tried to roll her eyes towards her. There was another short silence between them. Both were expressionless, just focussed looking. Bhoomi felt a kind of utter anxiety. Shortly afterward, he went towards her and wiped her mouth with his hand. He kissed her eyes, not speaking very much. Bhoomi felt holy as a shrine. Pranaviram knew how he felt about her. Just because he was left without words did not imply that he was not serious about love.

Bhoomi reaffirmed her love for Pranaviram in candid terms. *I am looking out of the window again, but I can feel his eyes on me, and I have the oddest yearning to turn towards him, to smell the perfume on his clothes and his breath. It's a romantic feeling I guess; that scent reminds me of contentment. I paused wondering for a moment what he would do if I turned to face him and kissed his mouth. I feel his body move. He inclines forward; bending down, he picks up the newspaper at my feet. Blood is throbbing in my head, my heart beating aloud. I am inquisitive to know whether what I'm seeing or feeling is accurate, imagination, or memory.*

Bhoomi felt a kind of undying bond with him and revealed the inside stories of her life, starting from slum life to life in many stoppages that remained a problematic proposition altogether. Except for his birthplace, that he was from Chennai, Pranaviram did not speak beyond. Hearing her past life, he became a little coarser and rougher and stood stunned around the edges. His face gave a severe look. He was wearing a soft brown shirt and sleeves, as always, pushed up his forearms and thin jeans. He was leaning against a column. Feet crossed at the ankles, a look that worried Bhoomi if she were wrong in intimating him about her rotten life. She covered her mouth with both hands, eyes stung with unshed tears. She stared at him, speechless. She was almost talking to herself, "It feels so weird to have disclosed all of that aloud."

Bhoomi took courage and told Pranaviram, "We need to make thoughtful decisions before we take the next step. I don't want to risk anyone's life unless necessary." Bhoomi's speech was met with an immediate chorus of support. Pranaviram's words glorified his love for Bhoomi in simple terms, "I know not what is going to happen to us; I only know we need to start our new life together as I believe your confession has given me the everlasting impression of purity of heart and magnanimity of your goals."

His words profoundly magnified his love, "With just a glance I am lucky that our friendship has grown into a true romance, thanking the road to the contagious hospital; as I decide to tie the nuptial knot and give my life a title."

His gratitude to life was evident in the words 'thanking the hospital' as it was the temple of their first meeting.

Marriage

Bhoomi was immensely happy to find a soul mate. Her love for Pranaviram had eventually emerged. Marriage was in her mind without knowing if love was dual-sided. Bhoomi had a deep craze for leading an everyday life wherein she could see herself in a close-knit family with her spouse and children. An unknown fear arose if it remained a dream never to be realised. The moment Pranaviram came, Bhoomi's nerves got shrunk. Any negativity would disastrously mar her future. To her utter amazement, Bhoomi's dream man asked her if she could favour him for a date. She jumped at the proposal and, in no time, dressed herself in a simply pretty manner. Pranaviram's eyes blurred, seeing the ethereal beauty of his fiancee. Few days later, they had decided to tie the knot. A simple ceremony was enough to help them tie the eternal nuptial knot.

The first post-marriage destination was Mangrol town in Junagadh, Gujarat. This was her first trip by train. Bhoomi's excitement knew no bounds.

They took a bus from Ahmedabad to Gondal, then a cab to Junagadh. The long journey was quite tedious, though Bhoomi was over-excited to meet his aunt, who happened to be the sole survivor in his family.

Bhoomi could also explore the historic alleyways of the city where old and new co-exist in often dramatic contrast. Her childhood memories knew no regional boundaries. Shantibai's teaching ideologies were perfect; they taught Bhoomi that equality is the epitome of all things on earth.

Bhoomi realised coming this far was only possible with her husband, Pranaviram. His aunt gave her a warm welcome. Bhoomi was awestruck when she saw her husband talking in the local tongue. The following day, Bhoomi witnessed a scene that greatly astounded her. Huge money was exchanged between Pranaviram and his aunt Amolika. Suspicions emerged but smilingly, Bhoomi thwarted her evil mind.

Vowed to spend days and nights together
Unholy, to perceive my man as a faker
If I smell something foul
I am the great grey owl.

The revelation of some unknown facts, namely, Pranaviram was not the actual owner of the medicine shop and that financial instability had almost ruined his fortune, made Bhoomi once and again bizarre, "Am I duped into travelling to Junagadh for some other inexplicable reasons?" Doubts apart, days rolled into weeks, then a month, and no love seemed lost between Bhoomi and her man, Pranaviram.

They had a pleasant bond until money reigned supreme in his mind one day. Pranaviram took her to a red light area without the knowledge of Bhoomi, fed her with enough edibles, and gifted her expensive gifts as well as if it were a farewell meeting. A minute stopped and Pranaviram was nowhere to be seen. Five ladies welcomed her with beautiful attire and gold-plated jewellery, she had hardly seen before. Somewhere down the lane, she wondered whether whoredom was her final destiny. Her belief in her man was bountiful; never could she imagine herself a part of a betrayal story. Two months lapsed, but there was no news of his arrival. In greater desperation, Bhoomi decided to find an escape route, "But every time I get caught, brutally assaulted physically, verbally, and even sexually. "

Bhoomi screamed aloud thinking of her destiny which betrayed her once more.

To you, Pranaviram, I surrendered my virginity
Alas it's a hamartia
I know not which will be my next city.
My leg is lowly good now, and lack of timely treatment has given me a permanent disability.
I am in another brothel in Gujarat
My soul is immensely hurt.

Bhoomi wanted to know the whereabouts of her husband if he was still alive. Her husband and his so-called aunt destroyed her imagination by selling her illegally to a brothel. But by a bout of good luck, an unknown pity arose in the mind of Rashi Shah, and she decided to shower ample kindness on her.

Bhoomi was not without suspicion, as life had taught her lessons enough. She now could segregate between evil and fair designs.

Life has manifold lessons to teach
It is we who do not want to come within its reach
Choose to be wise and not a fool
To be happy it's only the rule.

Introspective Journey

Bhoomi at times delved deep into her mind in the manner of knowing thyself and the world around.

Not allowing human beings to live at peace, and traversing beyond to trade with human flesh, can there be anything more gruesome and heinous a crime on earth?

No more wounds on human flesh
Lest the mother earth will bleed profusely
Her wrath can take the form of natural disasters
Bringing forth a doomsday or a final annihilation of mankind.

Bhoomi was at times restless but 'inner wisdom' had restored her to her real self once more.

None can unravel the mystery of this beautiful creation called 'life'. Men are born, but needless to know why they are born. He is on his way to complete his life tenure but, in reality, remains oblivion of life till the journey ends. He marches ahead with his success story but seldom ponders on the dilemma encircling his life, the goal towards which he is moving, whether that is the ultimate end, or whether life will offer him something different. What is the immediate next? The disciplinary forces almost loose significance in his mind mainly because man, through lack of faith or vision, has identified himself with the frightening figures of chaos.

What a piece of work is a man? The question arises as to whether this remark is still applicable to man. 'Reason' no longer seems to dominate man's decisions, as evident in his actions. There is an excellent transformation in man's mind set, not for the good but for the worst. Because man's mind is no longer within his domain, his actions do not correlate with his thought process.

The catastrophe that menaces man results from his thoughts and ideals. If he passively submits to the forces that have raised, he is calling for his destruction at his own hands. If there is one power that man possesses, it is his power to alter his way of life. A man shouldn't resign himself to the march of time and forfeit his freedom but should act as a free, creative being, ready to undertake any risks and responsibilities for the consequence of his act. He should, at his best, try to recover his creative powers.

Man's life is surrounded by various divergent problems that inevitably encounter and must be coped with. Nothing can undo what has already been done, but man at least has a chance to remake the future and make the world a better place to live in. He should also realize what it means to be a human being and that man has a significant contribution to make and the very act of understanding and acknowledging his potentialities might constitute an advance over what was gone before.

Thus, Bhoomi's long introspective journey was beautifully expressed in few words.

Entrap – 3

A few days later, Bhoomi was introduced to Mehul Choksi and his wife, a childless couple married for thirteen years. They eagerly asked Bhoomi if she could serve as a surrogate mother as they wanted to become parents once in their lifetime. Unable to decide, Bhoomi accepted the proposal after a short pause. Appreciations abound for Bhoomi, though it was an unknown concept for her.

The financial vulnerability, instability had given birth to surrogate mothers. Bhoomi was at the height of the depression.

I have lost all my emotional stability
How about helping a couple who is struggling with infertility.

Bhoomi agreed and finally decided to help a family come to life. But visiting hospitals seemed not a welcome idea for Bhoomi as corona waves still continued though a milder one. Nonetheless, she braved the circumstances. Bhoomi paused after hearing a conversation that Rashi Shah had maintained this business of providing surrogate mothers for the last five years. Suspicions arose as Bhoomi again heard Rashi saying to one of her assistants that she was having a flourishing business now that she used to sell the new-borns at a higher rates by falsely declaring that the babies were dead. Bhoomi couldn't digest this idea and immediately decided to report by dialling police helpline no. 100. The incident was over in one day, and it was successful in a few hours.

Thank you, God, for the courage you have given me to put a halt to this heinous crime.

Bhoomi's smiles came forth as never before. A few hours later, police arrested the mastermind, Rashi Shah, and her team for running the surrogacy racket; according to reports, they had sold around three hundred new born babies in the past five years, all were less than five months. The *rent–a–womb* industry, or instead 'baby factory', has been sealed forever in that district. It came as a great source of relief in the entire Gujarat.

Finally, Bhoomi got her independence in the real sense of the term, and no more prisons or hells awaited her.

I ask myself if it's the last dregs of the prison still hunting my veins, but something feels wrong with me today. My memories of my time in this frightening cell are suddenly too recent, settled significantly at the forefront of my mind. I thought I would be able to take out those haunting memories out of my head but no, here they are once again, dredged out of the darkness eighty four days in perfect mental agony. Nearly three months without access or outlet to the outside world. Very, very long without the warmth of good humans.

No more prison, no more hell
I am finally in my best self.

Shanti

Unknowingly for Bhoomi, good days were awaiting. Her courageous acts became popular in social media platforms. Delhi, Meerut and Gujarat police records had found Bhoomi as the saviour of thousands of kids and teenagers in Delhi and a reliever to hundreds of mothers in Meerut who had almost lost their sons in drug abuse cases. These valiant acts to name a few had enabled the police teams to put giant masterminds in captivity. A drug racket was unveiled; Shivani, the caretaker of the orphanage house, *Anath Ashram* and Rashi Shah, the owner of *Jamini Chatralaya* had been put behind the bars.

Awards adorned Bhoomi as never before. The Gujarat along with U.P and Delhi government had decided to donate Rupees one crore in recognition of her extraordinary courage to prevent Child trafficking, busting the local drug racket in Meerut and unearthing the surrogacy scam to name a few.

Bhoomi had decided to build her own organisation in New Delhi as a centre for rehabilitation, restoration of the survivors of trafficking girls and women in India.

Grandma, I am standing high on a pedestal.
So high, but alas!! I am unable to reach you
Your dogmas will always remain alive in me
To do good to humanity will be my gospel
Indeed, my goodness will serve as a sample
For all lives living on earth in its entirety.

Bhoomi had recruited few of rescued girls and women into her newly formed 'Shanti organisation' based in Shalimar Bagh, New Delhi. A website of her 'Shanti organisation' had also been launched. Her videos on YouTube had become viral in social media. Several organisations had joined her in freeing thousands of girls across India and abroad.

Girls from Kandla port in Gujarat who were travelling to Dubai were rescued. Again traffickers were arrested from Simdega district of Jharkhand, Andhra Pradesh, Kolkata, Assam to name a few. Many NGOs had offered women spies to aid Bhoomi in her new missions hereafter.

Tons of awards adorned Bhoomi; nevertheless, she was restless in rescuing thousands of Bhoomis. The prestigious award, 'Naari Paraakram' was bestowed on Bhoomi on the auspicious occasion of 'World Day against Trafficking in Persons.'

She revisited the slum where she had spent her childhood days and distributed foodstuffs amongst her family friends therein. Her friends could identify her at once; simultaneously spontaneous overflow of feelings of grief, and happiness betwixt her and time and again that she had a grand realisation that she had a wonderful family to look upon, enhanced her contentedness.

Older memories flashed in her mind, but Bhoomi moved on.

Only few lines had summed up her 'life cycle'.

I have a long mission, a vision to accomplish, I cannot wait and ponder as a huge onus lies on my shoulder.
My promise henceforth is to explore and restore the lives once destroyed
Only to give them the rightful place in the chain of beings
My life hereafter will be cause for many to rejoice
As I have vowed to reunite, 'long lost souls' with their kith and kin
It is a small step to wipe out all my sins
My mission is to set at liberty those who are oppressed
My rescue operation will reinstate the broken pieces once fragmented
No longer will they choose to walk down the wrong streets
My final promise is to take the 'once lost girls' on the path of ecstasies.

Korean Craze

None could stop Bhoomi from accomplishing the higher tasks of rescuing girls similarly encased with fake promises. Bhoomi was apprehensive that this project of rescuing humans involved abundant risk factors. She decided to take a different name altogether, 'Abhaya'.

Oh! How many times do I need to change myself and me?
The world needs a definition anew
Women's power needs it, too
Never undermine a girl
She is a powerhouse, a twinkling pearl.

After a few days, Bhoomi took a rather bold decision to remain as Bhoomi.

An unconquerable mind coupled with courage can never submit or remain subdued.

Her first venture was to make her video of recapturing and rehabilitating girls and women who were being trafficked and it went viral on social media. She approached several organisations to help her in this mission, 'Save Humans.' Bhoomi's Journey henceforth wore a noble tag embedded with many purposes, a way to give peace to many forlorn girls and kids. These poor beings were employed under hazardous circumstances in conditions wherein children in India are employed in the worst forms of child labour, including commercial sex exploitation, due to reasons obvious 'grave poverty.'

Traffickers used threats, fraud, physical and sexual violence, and even coerced substance to lure and manipulate their victims. They looked out for highly vulnerable, mainly desperate people and entice them with job offers, a chance to study abroad, or a chance of escaping poverty through the sale of body organs. Not all trafficking cases, started off with duplicity, deceit and falsehood many children, girls and women were captured, exploited, controlled, abused and impaired beyond repair.

Bhoomi was desperate to annihilate trafficking altogether from this world.

Bhoomi's words had sprung from her life's detestations.

Monster men live amongst us
Tearing the innocent souls into pieces
Bringing unnamed darkness around the earth
Our children are being kidnapped and enslaved, trafficked for the sex trade.
What can be more inhuman than turning young and old into a casket of broken spirits?
They are mercilessly sold to the highest bidder
Alas! The world has stooped so low

By perpetuation of heinous crimes
An act of barbaric Satan in the devil's shrines.

Bhoomi could recollect how she was safely taken out from Nadira's den to the exit route by Anya, her friend and a saviour. Bhoomi's tears had almost dried. Anya had narrated to Bhoomi the plight of girls in her village in Bihar. Every day, a girl went missing. The local police hardly cared and dared to know the real story behind the missing episodes. Suspicions grew alarmingly when locals were informed that some teenage boys and girls lost their lives in Corona and that the dead bodies were not allowed to be brought back home as the virus was deadly dangerous.

Anya, somehow reached Meerut in a similar way like that of her friend Bhoomi, though both were from other dwelling states. As an orphan, Anya had nothing to lose, leaving her hometown. Her tormenting journey from Bihar to Nadira's enclave was worth a phase never to relive again. The horrendous reality that the internal organs of the missing girls and boys were being sold, besides knowing that they were still alive, living elsewhere from where there was never a return journey, cumulatively made Anya leave her older memories wholly and start a new life entirely unknown. She was happy as a cook, filling her friends' tummy with yummy foods.

Henceforth, Bhoomi had geared up her mind to blow up all trafficking syndicates.

How hapless we become
Seeing the world order insane
How to unravel the sickening truth
When humanity has become so rude.

Bhoomi never viewed this world sceptically, as evident in her powerful words....

There is a beauty in microscopic existence
I continue my journey in a small hermitage
Trying to illuminate all in distress with great persistence
Almighty God, all we need is your assistance.

Mainly, Anya's story unnerved Bhoomi beyond imagination. She decided to keep Bihar as the top target state. Sitting in the Bihar railway station with few of her allies, Bhoomi's eyes caught a man, a father who was restless to find her daughter Rajni. Bhoomi had recently collaborated with the special operation teams for rescuing trafficked women.

Along with five girls, Rajni was last seen heading towards a movie hall. When enquired about her other friends, they were pretty clueless, as she and five others did not come to school that day. From sources, Mr. Shreeram, the father of the girl, came to know that his daughter was crazy about everything Korean, and five more girls who were missing were staying in a boarding school. A day ago, they went to their local guardian's house. Mr. Shreeram, showed his utmost concern for all the missing girls.

As per research done by Bhoomi, she understood the whole scenario. *Korean pop music has been receiving a fair amount of global attention lately. The recent soap opera sensation has reignited the Korean wave across East Asia. Korean dramas took India by storm. The quest to understand a nation's greatness remains always alive. The ascent from a poverty ridden country to one of the top economic powers is a complex proposition. This 'miracle' on the Han River attracts youngsters from India to visit this wonderful country.*

The lost jewellery amply proved that Rajni had sold all of them only to move to Korea. From one of the diaries recovered, it was found that a travel agent from Bodh Gaya would act as their pathfinder to South Korea.

Bhoomi contacted the Delhi police commissioner, and immediately, under the intervention of the Ministry of Home Affairs, an LOC, Look Out Circular was issued. Accordingly, a tip-off was passed on to CISF and all airport security to thoroughly check and stop all South Korean outbound passengers. All six girls were rescued, and a major international human trafficking racket was foiled.

Bhoomi was also successful in the rescue operations in Bahadurganj, Bihar. She was pleased to save girls with a relatively small network who were in the dungeon of horrifying human traffickers.

My humanitarian organisation would henceforth embark on new changes and take up new challenges to help establish a principled country by normalizing past abnormal practices. It will create a prosperous society where everyone can enjoy a decent life and cultural opportunities without anxiety and make a better nation adorned with jobs and economic vitality.

Such was Bhoomi's humbleness, when she said, "We will closely listen to all the voices of people and immediately take follow-up measures."

The fact that Bhoomi knew some titbits of the local language helped her unearth many a significant Trafficking cases. Slices of terrifying episodes of how girls had been entangled in different enticing acts got unveiled in many ghastly operations.

Some three hundred more girls were rescued from Seemanchal region of Bihar who had been entrapped with variegated promises. In a way, the women trafficking racket was busted with a reinvigorating force that was hitherto unseen. Rightly or wrongly, Bhoomi had admitted that Anya's dreadful tales had energised her in the rescue mission with a promise to safe now or never.

Rescue Operation

Bhoomi's next target destination was Chhattisgarh. Girls here were sold in other states where rich zamindars, unmarriageable men that were older and disabled, used to marry minors. An eerie silence prevailed in the entire district of Raipur. The men and womenfolk remained silent lest their lives might be in danger. Hundreds of men and women operated as agents and suppliers to facilitate marriage with brides in other states at a cheaper rate.

Fourteen years old girl Manshi was kidnapped from Raipur district. Her whereabouts remained unknown. Bhoomi took the aid of the local people. The two friends, Manshi and Jhanvi were just a mile apart at the time of the kidnapping. The taxi driver was uttering words like Ambala and Hisar and Jhanvi heard it clearly. Bhoomi was sure about the place where Manshi got trapped. Jhanvi just gave Bhoomi taxi's registration number, enough for Bhoomi to start the rescue operation. Through this RC number its owner was traced.

Local police in Pathankot interrogated the owner and driver, and finally, the flat where Manshi and seventy more girls were forcefully kept in captivity in that four-storeyed building was rescued.

The girls were waiting for further selling and negotiation. Multiple gunmen guarded the flat. The operation was carried in the midnight hours. On seeing police personnel, gunmen started random firing. In retaliation, police overpowered those gunmen. Finally, all gunmen succumbed to the bullet injuries. Four Prime accused from Pokhra, Nepal were taken into custody. Manshi and the whole stock of girls were saved from those predators.

Minors are getting trapped
I need to be their rescuer, their ultimate comrade.

Manshi was finally rescued, and though she was asked to relocate to her hometown, Manshi rejected the plan of shifting back home. She only said, "I don't like being answerable to my society, ample queries will make me lose my vitality."

Too many questions would only thwart her desire to live life. Bhoomi tried to reassure her of the sound-knit protection their relatively small organisation would offer, ranging from keeping her name a secret to relocating her to a new job near her hometown. Bhoomi said in a tone that could be termed as a peaceful one, but hardly audible accepting life as it came.

I am humans' protector, life giver
I think there is nothing to shiver
People repose their immense faith in me
Their pathways will henceforth be renewed.

Bhoomi got troubled seeing minors getting trapped in many marriage trafficking cases which were mainly an attack on the rights of 'little lives' to live life freely in this beautiful abode called earth. The term 'beautiful' had lost all its significance in Bhoomi's terminology as she could only see 'chaos in this cosmos.'

Bhoomi desperately murmured, "Once trafficked, women become ostracised from society, making their rehabilitation far more complicated."

Bhoomi would sometimes let her mind speak words which was audible to the open sky above and earth beneath.

A bright or a darker future of the nation rest on the youths of today's world.
The misdirected youths are cutting the vitals of the society and eating away its roots.

Bhoomi's words showed anger, no other means to procure a secured future, the unemployed youths searched easy alternative means and once found consider it as an ultimate reward.

Manshi felt short of words to appreciate Bhoomi.

Bhoomi blessed all the rescued girls and even tried to enhance their knowledge of the realities of life. She narrated to all who were saved from that entrapped house, "Life is a series of decision and one wrong decision can ruin a life. To save the society from further deterioration, the family should not shirk away from the serious responsibility of acting as a pathfinder to its members when they find themselves encircled in a horrifying dilemma. Even the youth needs to be reminded that there is something above personal profit, something above of life, which can give a joy more perennial and everlasting. In these days of deepening cleavages between anxiety for the future, the family should play a major role in easing the tension and understanding each other's way of life, and in the process must understand that the misdirected passions of the young generation cannot be curbed by hungry words but by right inspirational words which must arise from the family itself, and that the youth must utilize their talent not only in the hope of doing something beneficial to themselves but also of doing something beneficial to mankind and in the process will be paid by posterity itself."

Bhoomi was more concerned with rehabilitating the trafficked girls, and bringing them to their earlier self in a manner that was quite appreciable. Bhoomi vehemently believed only lessons about realities of life would give those girls a reason to live life alive.

Woman safety laws have been framed to infuse a feeling of security in the hearts of millions of women by safeguarding their interest too. But a question arises of how far it has succeeded because, according to some, the gross reality seems somewhat different. On one side, it is seen that women who feel that men have committed atrocities have not been able to rise in violence despite the protection of these acts, which may be due to a lack of courage and confidence and primarily due to a lack of belief in themselves. So, some feel that the present scenario of women is that they are dominated and devoid of facilities available to men. But the other phase of women is that they have outnumbered men in most of the fields. So, the present state of women is apparent. On one side, they are powerless to come to power; on the other, they are full of immense potentialities that have become synonymous with power.

Ramlila Ground

Back in New Delhi, Bhoomi could witness people, all in festive rood as if the inanimate things were brought to life. Dussehra was celebrated yearly in the Ramlila grounds in a way that seemed larger than life itself.

Every year, the effigies of Ravan, the ten-headed demon king of Lanka, are burnt to ashes with explosives that sounds louder than thunderstorms. Every year, the grounds near Ajmeri gate, where the maidan is currently located, played host to Ramlila jubilation, the story of how lord Ram, king of Ayodhya, vanquished Ravan in the battle of Lanka, which Hindus believe is the story of the triumph of good over evil. The sounds of the explosives will be even audible in the narrow lanes of old Delhi. Hundreds throng to the main ground; some are dressed as gods, some like demons again, others like Ram and some like Hanuman, and their faces are painted orange, red devils with black faces all in their fullest merriment to participate in the grand celebrations. The effigies of demons, namely Ravan, Meghnad, and Kumbhakaran, are as high as a fortress, all in the way of their final demolition.

Bhoomi was happy to relive life again under the open sky, and again, she recalled her dark days in the dungeon with its humming walls. She took out her rather fashionable new smartphone, which she decided to use to the best of her purposes. She looked at the mirror; her face lacked a definition of beauty.

Is it reminiscent of something most faded and outworn, frail and tilted, or that it signifies nothing?

Quickly, she regained her senses, "Beauty is never in faces but in works that are remembered for ages."

She recollected her grandma's words echoing and re-echoing in her ears.

Never let yourself get lost in the vales of oblivion; appear larger than the common masses. Draw attention to yourself by carving a niche that has to be unforgettable and sometimes controversial. To create a crowd, you must perform somewhat different and odd deeds. General mobs are magnetically attracted toward unusual and inexplicable.

Bhoomi, the hazel-eyed girl undeterred by what life had offered her, proudly declared herself as the proud possessor of an 'indisputable winning mentality'.

Present well lived makes every past a dream of happiness and every future a vision of hope.

Bhoomi's maturity could handle attention. Bhoomi's motto, in a nutshell, was to be among crowds, serving them and lifting them to the plane of a civilized human being. Bhoomi summed up the festivities in a few words, which signified her understanding of the stories of great histories and mythologies.

Dussehra is a festival to rejoice
Our life's course is our choice
The restoration of truth, the conquest of good over evil
Is there anything more to unveil?

All of a sudden Bhoomi fell into the abode of imagination, her usual home during lonely hours. That time some conflicting thoughts came to her mind in relation to a woman, especially her dilemmas.

A woman's mind is torn by some invisible, indefinable emotional conflict so that life outside his mind is merely a dream life, a far-off vision seen in a mirror, and the beautiful images are only her faint shadows of authentic self. She is torn into a dilemma. She is aware of having lost contact with the real world. While trying to know others, she tends to forget herself.

A sense of isolation, loneliness, and no help from any corner haunts the minds of modern women. The conflicting passions disturb her emotional state so much that she tends to lose her identity.

The dilemma of modern women will prevail so long as the vexed problems of the word remain. As voices of the new generation, we can shape and modify the structure of society from the experience we have gathered by living among people whose lives are full of a multitude of purposes. So, life is but an accumulation of experiences. If that is life, experience makes life what it is. Life and death-in-life have become two synonymous terms. We should make life alive by making it lively, by making this dwelling place a place worth living.

Dubai Encounter

Travel agents allegedly selling women from Uttar Pradesh to Arab sheikhs in Gulf countries were arrested, and a vast trafficking racket was busted. Bhoomi aided the Rachakonda police force to extract all the secret information related to the agency named 'Journey to Heaven.'

Spies were employed to follow the footsteps of suspected travelling agents. Fake travel agents had lured hundreds with phony jobs in Dubai, Kuwait, to name a few, in exchange for lakhs of money and near entrapment at the other end.

Bhoomi had engaged village heads or *sarpanch* to keep track of these agencies operating mainly from home. The particular travel agency, 'Journey to Heaven' had confiscated the passports of all women, and thus, the unending tale of misery began. Never too late, Bhoomi was even more successful in this horrific mission.

I can give a clear picture of hollowing images of fraud.

Even though Bhoomi was heckled and threatened at the roadside by jeeps with black glasses, she dared to walk the pathways bravely. The head sarpanch house was gheraoed from all sides by her team of women who had once been trapped in similar cases as he seemed to have links with various fake travel and tour operators. Kingpin details had been disclosed. Bhoomi was en route to Dubai, "This is my first journey abroad, help me my Lord."

She contacted Aziza Abdel, head of the 'Al-Hasan Foundation for Woman and Children', who helped Bhoomi and her organisation achieve a stronger foothold in Dubai. Bhoomi collaborated with anti-trafficking model task forces in Dubai, who devised comprehensive action plans to capture the culprits locally and internationally.

Bhoomi put forth a picture of reality.

Innocent women are enticed to attractive jobs and become sex slaves under Arab sheikhs in gulf cities. How cruel is the reality?

Satyam Singh, the head agent, was forcibly captured by a special operation team for running the ring on behalf of seven travel agents in Dubai. Al Baraha area of Dubai was raided, and heads of brothels were charged with women trafficking, and traffickers were sentenced to life imprisonment. Dubai Anti-trafficking Task Force were mainly involved in this mission.

Finally, a sense of enormous relaxation dawned on me.

I am immensely happy now, seeing around five hundred forty educated trafficked women released from Dubai who have been exploited physically and mentally for years.

Bhoomi said to Aziza Abdel, "As a human rights activist, I have sometimes failed to comprehend the moral doctrine of human rights. The clandestine nature of these heinous crimes has enveloped the general masses in total darkness. I have gained extensive confidence after this successful venture was carried out in Dubai. Many international organisations have called for collaboration."

Bhoomi's joy knew no bounds.

My words simply fall short to explain their painful hearts.

Bhoomi's eyes had reddened thinking what man had made of man.

The flesh trade had been brutally carried on with customers in the Middle- East, and the slave markets in New Delhi, Mumbai, and Kolkata remained the transit point for these sex traffickers. The traveller's documents were verified and scrutinized at the immigration desks at airports, so the sex agents have found it difficult to deport 'trafficked humans' quickly. Instead, trafficking agents have started sending these unfortunate lot of people first to Thailand, morocco, Bangkok, and Sri Lanka and obtained visas for Middle Eastern countries such as Kuwait, Saudi Arabia, Dubai, and Egypt, to name a few. Africa had gained a new demoralized status of being a slave market with buyers mainly from Tanzania and Kenya. The Modus operandi of perpetrators of sex slaves remained 'deception', and 'debt bondage' is primarily involved.

Bhoomi spoke in candid terms to Chief of Dubai Task Force about the grave realities, "Human trafficking is one of the most brutal crimes against humanity, a gross commercialisation of human flesh and a sordid defeat of rights too."

I am happy that my real name and identity has given me a pacified self.

Bhoomi's actions were synonymous with the word *fearlessness*, her actions would be an acumen of careful precision and strategic actions.

She solidly believed, "To protect oneself, we must be as fluid and flexible as water. By taking a definite shape and having a visible plan ahead, we are only open to attack."

Bhoomi, from the earlier times, showed her originality only with her 'tolerant friends' who appreciated her uniqueness and genuine boldness.

Chhath Puja

Chhath puja is a vibrant and energetic festival celebrated in the northern states of Bihar, Jharkhand, and Chhattisgarh. It has high cultural and religious significance. Celebrated with great ardour, Chhath puja falls in the lunisolar month of Kartik. Surya, the sun god, is worshipped with the highest devotion. Due to my days of captivity, I have not felt its fervour.

Bhoomi many a times took refuge in the world of imagination which gave her a sense of belonging.

Sometimes, I used to stay restless for days counting the cracks in the walls, the threads in the blanket, individual hairs on my head, and the number of minutes I can hold my breath. Cumulatively, I am just a living idol, but I wish for the one thing I have always wanted, I wish all the time for a grand Chhath puja, wherein I can seek blessings from Surya god. Chhath puja is here. Let's celebrate; my mind has though become ravaged.

Bhoomi took the chance to speak to the organisers of Chhath puja in Delhi, "Seeing the survivors of trafficking girls and women in utter agony and plight, my world has collapsed inwardly. I will not rest until my purpose is served. I will be the saviour of humankind henceforth."

All of a sudden, there was a massive onrush of emotion.

I hope Lord Surya has not forgotten to bless my mission.

Shantibai used to relate stories of Chhathi Bai, the protector goddess of children. The feeling of elation at the thought that without 'corona' general mass could also worship sun-god with spiritual fervour made her somewhat positive.

I will miss the handmade delicacies of my grandma
Kheer, roti and thekua
Nevertheless, my mind is at peace
Rescuing girls, women and kids, the mission which I will never
cease.

Bhoomi talked to one of the old women, Anjaliji about present scenario of youths. "*I am worried about the new generation youths who had gone almost misdirected,* Bhoomi shared the *prasads,* showering all her blessings on new generation youths.

Bhoomi's thoughts on life's maze was simply amazing.

Nothing can undo the violence that the youths commit. But we have the power to redesign the future. Only right inspiration can help to give our world a stronger hold and give its foundation a sturdy built. But a question arises what or rather who can be the most reliable fountain head of inspiration.

Bhoomi showed her expertise in worldly affairs in few words.

The days ahead are beset with innumerable strifes
My promise is to save many human lives.

UNODC

The United Nations Office on Drugs and Crime (UNODC) had arranged a global conference on combatting human trafficking in Vienna to celebrate World Day against trafficking in persons on 30th July. The conference witnessed the active participation of most of the global anti-trafficking organisations.

I am happy 'Shanti organisation' had made its international presence.

Members of three anti - trafficking organisations of India accompanied Bhoomi on this Journey. Ms. Laila wonderfully interpreted Bhoomi's points of view in English to the delegates in UNODC.

I am not so proficient in English, my heartfelt thanks to Ms Laila for putting my thoughts and actions into words so stylish.

One additional plus point of this conference was that there would be an arms and combat training for all rescue activists. Training would be conducted by a private training institute. Bhoomi arrived in that conference along with her assistant ground activists. She knew her innate potentialities would be ennobled further more.

The international exposure was indeed taken as a 'blessings from Almighty' by Bhoomi. She took it as a chance to describe the deplorable condition of traumatized and dehumanised victims of trafficking in India.

Bhoomi spoke to Nigerian Human Activist Okunola, "The survivors of trafficking are key participants in all human related trafficking. We should give them the proper place in our society." Bhoomi voiced some sensitive issues to Argentines Sara Susana, "The period from rescuing to restoring a woman or a girl takes a much longer time in India, whereas in the U.K. it takes only 45 days at the most. Survivors in India have to carry the stigma and taboo relatively longer than other countries."

In the Vienna conference of UNODC, Bhoomi made certain draft proposals, "Mainly after victims have been rescued, their recovery period should be faster enough to build up self-determination and assimilate with the society easily. From forced labour to sex trafficking, any form of human trafficking should not be tolerated. For building self-confidence of the rescued womenfolk, foremost task is to create employment in respective countries. So there should be a resolution and it needs to be followed by all 193 countries and that respective governments and private industries, public sector companies, MNC'S, small scale industries have to keep some portion of job reservation for these rescued victims. These job reservation records should be commonly shared with UNODC's central server. Last but not the least rescued victims are the key players for fighting the traffickers and trafficking syndicates. So these rescued victims should be involved in all kinds of strategic tasks planned in UNODC level or whenever any of the member countries develop any kind of anti-trafficking action plan."

May be my core points are unheard by some but if carefully studied it can be a great testament too.

After the draft resolution in in UNODC, all activists had undergone combat arms training in Euro Tactical Training Institute. All activists had learned uses and live applications of various arms, sharp weapons training plus hand to hand combat training.

Bhoomi henceforth vowed to rescue and restore the trapped girls and women anywhere in the world.

Rehabilitating the fractured life of the traffickers remains my prime objective, besides giving psychological and mental support to them. I have fully supported this venture. I hope developing rehabilitation policies for the survivors of trafficking will only help them to get their final emancipation.

Bhoomi soon thereafter transported herself to the land of thoughtfulness only to encounter grave realities of life. Again her happiness in attending international conferences and meeting international friends was immense.

Life is not a dilemma but a solution. Once we understand the fact that not life but we women are in a gutter, we should also devise ways to get out of it, which can only be possible by interacting with people, by trying to know more about each other's culture, etc. so that need for social interaction, the idea of closeness should once again arise in the minds of people. It is only then that the dilemma will turn into a solution.

International conferences have helped me to explore multi-dimensional aspects and thereby make international friends. I always thank my grandma, who taught me the definition of human collaboration and, most importantly, the ways of this world. I can remember every word of my grandma and her efforts to make me a civilised human being.

Salma Reappears

I, Bhoomi miss you every day
As time goes by
If you get lost in your way
Be sure to recall me in every way.

Salma came to my mind many times. My feelings have been hidden in the subconscious. I can feel some numbness, the voice of the drizzle outdoors as if brought with it some serene melodies.

Shanti organisation received a call. Bhoomi prompted to one of the office assistants, "An international call, a muted voice from Colombia, perhaps a wrong one, we are in India."

Twice or thrice, Bhoomi shouted to know the caller's identity, but in vain.

The following call was more straightforward, but Bhoomi could hear only voices of tears. An hour later, two more calls came in a row but suddenly disconnected.

Bhoomi paused for a while and took a cup of 'Assam Chai', which rejuvenated her evermore.

A kind of nameless dread encompassed me once I heard the voice of Salma. There was an onrush of emotions. Only trying to assure Salma with few words that were in stock. I know we're close to finding the truth. It was Salma's voice from Uraba, Colombia.

I feel something weird, I feel uneasy.
Mind blogging incidents have almost eaten most of my vitals.

Bhoomi just couldn't help feeling, that the truth would be terrible. Bhoomi said in a rather desperate way to one of the fellow activists, Sanya, "I can't reply anymore because my mind has gone somewhere."

Suddenly, I feel a bit frightened and confused.
The Gulf of Uraba is one of the most dangerous places on earth
Once gone, never to return, can it be a mirth?

Bhoomi's state of mind became quite unstable and perplexed.

I have been thinking all day about Salma, her boldness of speech, and how time had something different in its list. I couldn't see her fearsome expression at that distance, but I felt she was alone, more than lonely. My phone rings in my pocket, making me terrified; my heart is pounding aloud as I reach for the phone. I know it will be nothing good either, and suddenly it stops. I was indeed right this morning when I felt that dread. I did not know what I had to be afraid of. I can't stand it. I wouldn't say I like waiting for the phone to ring. When the phone rings, what will it be? Will it be the worst news? Or will it be something most unexpected? Will I be able to find her? Every day, every hour that passes, I become more certain. Salma will be one of those names; hers will be one of those stories, lost, missed, body never found.

Bhoomi's loss was apparent, there was a kind of perennial agony. Nothing could be more painful than feeling utter helplessness in rescuing a friend whose life remained in the ocean of uncertainty.

The screen on my phone is blank. Arrogantly blank. No text messages, no missed calls. Every time I look at it, I feel betrayed by 'lady luck'. The breath caught in my throat, and I couldn't speak. I walked around the desk and leaned against it. I wanted to scream aloud.

Bhoomi was determined to accomplish this 'Mission Colombia' and bring Salma and all her friends back to India.

Pledged to safeguard innocent souls
That remains my ultimate goal
Though a challenging, onerous role
It is only myself, to console.

Sources revealed that Uraba is a region in northwest Colombia, a dense jungle on the Caribbean coast. Its towering rainforest trees serve as a fortress for the world's most dangerous criminals. Uraba is connected to Port Town Turbo and Medellin by road; these are only connections to the world outside. Uraba is famous as an anarchic, lawless region. The barely crossable jungle of Uraba is home to Urabenos leaders. Such a dangerous track, will I be able to hack?

Bhoomi was down with a terrible kind of dilemma.

The Gaitanistas, also known as the Gulf Clan, Urabenos, and Gaitanist Self-Defense Forces of Colombia, had risen from the embers of Colombia's paramilitary movement to become the dominant criminal force in Colombia, that has its command far beyond. Drug traffickers hold in high regard the Urabenos in the northwestern region of Colombia near the Panamanian border as it offered access to the Caribbean and Pacific coasts from the departments of Antioquia and Choco. Referring to itself as the Gaitanist Self-Defense Forces of Colombia, it was also called the Gulf Clan by the Colombian government.

I know information will help me to dig the innermost tunnels of some of the most wretched places on earth.

The group controlled druga making zones, trafficking corridors, and international dispatch points throughout north Colombia, along the Pacific and Atlantic coasts, and the land bordering Venezuela.

Bhoomi's voice reverberated with abundant positivism as she spoke to Sanya, "I have known all this because I have spent yesterday doing my ultimate research."

Bhoomi soon remained undeterred by those 'inhumane human rights' violators encompassing the innocent humans.

Never underrate the innate potentiality of a woman.
I must act impulsively, lest procrastination will lead to a catastrophe.

Mission Colombia

Rescate de Mujer, Red Capitulus, Liberacion sueno ECD, Bogat Columbia and Fuerzas De Coalition Por La Mujer were the organisations assisting 'Mission Colombia'.

Bhoomi received a call from her two old friends too besides Salma, who were captive in Uraba. Drug lords had similarly detained them along with Salma in Uraba, Antioquia region. They had been used as sex slaves. Around 1,200 girls and women were trafficked from about 13 countries: Albania, Greece, Uzbekistan, Morocco, Cameroon, India, Malaysia, Myanmar, Hungary, Canada, etc. Bhoomi's friends had requested to rescue them from this grave captivity. They were imprisoned under heavily armed guards with AKs.

Bhoomi had contacted anti-trafficking activists in all these countries. Those girls and women had been kept in highly animal-like conditions in a tiny room, and hundreds had been held captive. They had been regularly drugged. They had forced sex with many drugs producing people, armed guards, top drug mafia leaders, and managers.

Bhoomi formed a multinational activist task force. She took the help of five anti-trafficking organisations in Colombia. 'Bogat Colombia' was the organisation Bhoomi had known it well at the international conference held in Vienna. Four more humanist groups collaborated with Bhoomi in that rescue mission.

Bhoomi contacted the U.S. Department of Justice (DOJ) and discussed the modus operandi to recover all these multinational women and girls. On receiving the video footage from the joint activists forum in Colombia led by Bhoomi, the U.S. Department of Justice and the U.S. Department of State immediately decided to evacuate the victims. Bhoomi agreed that a joint operation of U.S. Navy Seals and Colombian SOF would be against the Uraba drug lords. The Uraba location was heavily guarded as it was in the midst of highly dense rainforest. So, a special operation was carried out with US Navy Seals.

Though I am stationed at the base I can easily see the maze.

In Bhoomi's words Salma stood for 'All women in turmoil'. It was decided that all the women activists from different countries would also go with Special Task Forces. Operation Colombia was tough. The task force consisted of 250 Colombian operation forces (SOF), 15 Navy Seals, and daredevil woman rescue activists, Bhoomi was among them. They formed a command centre at the Uraba coastal base station. They had used nine black hawks.

Nothing can be called mission impossible
Nothing on earth can be untraceable.

The geography of Uraba was non-navigable and full of dense rainforests. Rain forests had been edged with touch cliffs. Urabenos leaders were highly equipped to handle the rough conditions. Operation had been continued for several weeks. One helicopter crashed. The Urabenos guerrillas had engaged snipers at various strategic locations. They were heavy arms like RPGs, anti-aircraft guns, M24 sniper rifles, etc. Bhoomi was already well trained in military skills.

Salma is an embodiment of every woman who have been encased
Hunting the terrorist out will not be a wild goose chase
Winning the warfare has always remained my craze
That's the way how on earth I will leave my trace.

Both sides had been continuously engaged in heavy fights for several weeks. After they were airborne, ISR (Intelligence, Surveillance, and Reconnaissance) had been used to track down trafficking routes of guerrilla groups.

Bhoomi spoke to the operation commander, "We have broken the criminal rings that trafficked these womenfolk into forced prostitution or as slave workers. Now, the enormous task ahead is that all victims have been segregated and deported to their respective countries."

Meanwhile, Bhoomi was stationed in the coastal base control. After clearing the route, Bhoomi and other Colombian rescue activists proceeded to the victims' shelters. Still, gun fights were continuing. The first four layers of guerrilla covers had been demolished, and the last two layers still were giving their resistance to the Navy Seals and Colombian SOFs. Bhoomi was carrying a P228 pistol.

Miserably, she found Salma and two of her friends along with seven others had been killed in the crossfire. Others had been rescued.

My dear Salma, I have risked my life only to see you

With tearful eyes I bid adieu.
I bask in glory rescuing many
Alas! Without you my life has become lonely.

Bhoomi had clearly demonstrated that friendship 'knows no religion, knows no nationality'.

Bhoomi could transgress risking her life as she had the nobility and genuineness of purpose in mind.

Felicitation and Elevation

All these 13 anti-trafficking activists had been specially invited to the U.S. They had received special funding of more than usd 250 million, out of that usd 180 million had been given to all the victims. Twelve activists each got usd 5 million; Bhoomi especially received usd 12 million as a lead whistle-blower. Bhoomi had been honoured with the highest U.S. medal for 'extraordinary valour' in the White House by the U.S. Secretary of State for her extraordinary contribution towards combating human trafficking in Colombia.

Bhoomi had formulated a strategic plan, which was the first of its kind on the subject of human trafficking in Indian cities. Her efforts were not restricted to India alone. She thought of herself as a world citizen, trying to serve Mother Earth in the days to come.

Bhoomi had received a tumultuous welcome at IGI airport. The organisation named 'Shanti' was elevated to a plane of ultimate exultation.

The honourable minister for Women and Child Development, India convened a special meeting. In her speech, she praised Bhoomi for the extraordinary courage exhibited during the Colombia expedition, the Dubai mission, and many more rescue operations in India. She said, "Bhoomi's mission exemplifies 'Women Empowerment' at its best. Unless human trafficking gets eliminated from this earth, we will not rest." Bhoomi thanked the WCD ministry for the words of appreciation and encouragement.

A special All India Anti-human trafficking ceremony was organized under the Ministry of Human Affairs and Social Justice and Empowerment. Bhoomi was felicitated. The esteemed 'Nari Shakti' award, the much coveted one, was conferred upon Bhoomi by the Honourable President of India at the Rashtrapati Bhavan. National and international awards and felicitation ceremony only heightened her spirits to work with more dedication to save women in distresses.

Hollywood producer cum director Henry Harrington had shown keen interest in making a movie on Bhoomi's biography. Henry Harrington flew to Delhi and met Bhoomi officially. They had discussed the plots and the entire film's project.

It would be a biopic based on Bhoomi's entire journey of life from living in a slum to becoming a human activist. The film would also shed light on triumphant mission undertaken by Bhoomi on the most dangerous trafficking zones of the earth.

The entire movie project would cost around usd 300 million. Julia Hanks will be in the lead role of Bhoomi, in the upcoming Hollywood movie entitled as **SLUM GOD BILLIONAIRE.** A 'life right agreement' had been finalised between Bhoomi and Walt Paramount Pictures and Bhoomi had received usd 80 million.

In an interview with CNN and major TV news channel of India, Bhoomi was seen quite jubilant at the entire project. She said, "I am confident that this big budget film will be blockbuster and hit all national and international theatres. I am again happy to announce that entire money will be distributed in the various anti-human trafficking organisation in India who work for the rehabilitation of the rescued girls and women which will include their education too."

Minutes paused and just then a call came, "It's an international call, a call from Egypt. We are in India................."

Author's Note

Lost Humanity-an attempt at resurrection

A man boasting of his latest technological know-how becomes a nullifying acumen of knowledge when his action speaks something other. He goes on with his actions until his quest brings an array of resentment in others. A child may lose his conception of the world before he or she grows up. His life gets encircled in a horrifying maze; breaking through it becomes at times a difficult proposition and is just left with vague images equating nothingness. Thus, reflecting on child trafficking, a modern form of slavery that dissects the child into many crippled slices. Nearly 30 million people are living in dehumanising cells across the globe, acts amounting to deep violation of human rights. Within the embryo of human trafficking lies the child trafficking which seemingly is the gravest form of human exploitation, the acceleration of its growth has been minimized to a considerable length though. Child trafficking in the words of UNICEF is "Any person under 18 who is recruited transported, harboured or received for the purpose of exploitation either within or outside a country."

India knowingly or unknowingly is a transit country for child traffickers. Children born to poverty have remained vulnerable and even inter- country trafficking has become the last resort to survival. Hesitatingly forced labour, beggary and brothels become their way of life. An invisible workforce and lack of proper legislation remain the cause of ongoing exploitation of child maids in India as claimed by ILO (International Labour Organisation). It is a blatant disregard for the dignity of human being. Stories of child escaping their violent pimp are not just roadside resonances but are cries of a painful heart urging every living soul to become proactive now and not until when someone they knew falls prey to the crime. Worldwide supportive services have come to voice their grievances by blocking the tunnels of this heinous crime. Global initiative to trap the traffickers is a bold step indeed. Children are the hope of mankind and improving their quality is a prerequisite for the cumulative development of a nation. Mother Teresa aptly voiced "It's not how much we give but how much love we put into giving." Mechanisms to ensure the healthy development of work impacting children's protection needs to be installed at various child rehabilitation centres. Reports say that 24000 children are rescued each year in Delhi .Again tea garden labourers of Assam are being continuously misled by illegal placement agencies thus giving them a temporary respite not too long the reality comes to the fore.

Child traffickers should be met with stringent punishments. According to recent statistics nearly 3.6 million children have been forced into domestic child labour by placement agencies. An alarming concern is the rising inflow of children from domestic labour to sexual exploitation. Nearly 60% of them are from Bihar and Assam, Jharkhand Chhattisgarh .Most of them are young girls and they face different forms of exploitation by their employers. Girls of the age group between 14- 17 years are trafficked into sex trade every year. A huge revenue is generated by each brothel through child sexual exploitation each year. It is indeed a grave reality: a layer, a stratum of society has been fractured with pictures so morbid that imagining their life creates a kind of fear psychosis. Trafficking mainly of children is an undercover criminal offence. The problem needs to be discussed at a deeper level with strict imposition of punishment on the criminals. Most Trafficked children are victims of fraud, deception, misuse, of power and lack of awareness regarding their basic human rights. A database of trafficked children need to be maintained on a more disciplined and a regular basis. A need to train the parents of the under developed arenas is of utmost importance as in most cases it is they who send their wards to far off places just to secure a lucrative future for them. Children's security should be given prime importance in formulating state budgets.

Human trafficking has been slowly entrenched in the socio-economic and the cultural domain as a complex phenomenon. The underprivileged girls, women, children are its victims. They are trafficked beyond India to Thailand, Myanmar, Vietnam, China, and Middle -East and the lists go on. Informal friendly networks and highly organised criminal networks some even posing as religious organisations pave the way for the culprits as they share a part in facilitating the traffickers. Survey also speaks that traffickers may also be the fake employment agencies, gurus of religious sects, massage parlours, NGO'S and shockingly even doctors and lawyers specialising in adoption cases. Trafficking is a predatory behaviour. In corona days people who were most vulnerable to trafficking and at risk were the children, girls and women refugees .Indeed covid-19 signalled a complete human disaster and a sudden availability of potential prey. The covid induced recession ushered in an aura of uncertainty, financial instability leading to large scale trafficking.

Commendable efforts were made by UNODC to stop criminal traffickers to take undue advantage of pandemic and exploit the vulnerable .According to a global report on trafficking in persons launched by UNODC women and girls were trafficked for sexual exploitation and boys were trafficked in corona times mostly for forced labour.

Human trafficking or flesh trade is a rather difficult hypothesis. Trafficking is done for reasons obvious: sexual exploitation, forced labour, forced begging to name a few, at times through depth-based coercion, fraud, deception, abduction all for the purpose of human exploitation. In the post covid times, national and international media coupled with law enforcement agencies are working hard to crack down the proliferation of criminally run enclaves around the globe.

The counter trafficking data collaborative is the first global data hub on human trafficking with data contributed by organisations around the world. UNODC surveys government on trafficking victims identified in their respective countries for the Global report on Trafficking in Person, using a common set of questions with a standard set of index and thus accumulates the results..

Global estimates of Modern Slavery, Forced Labour and Forced Marriage is a global estimate of prevalence of human trafficking related crimes of forced labour and forced marriage produced by the International Labour Organisation (ILO), International Organisation for Migration (IOM) and Walk Free Foundation (WFF).

The European Commission had put forth EU growth map to fight drug trafficking and organised crime by setting out 17 solid actions aimed at demolishing criminal networks and collaborating with international partners to annihilate trafficking altogether.

Onus lies on us to impart fullest knowledge to the vulnerable communities about the abuses that trafficking victims suffer and how the human trafficking cases have dramatically escalated in recent years. In the absence of comprehensive anti-trafficking legislation, the ongoing detention and deportation of trafficking victims will continue. Government sponsored services for all trafficked humans namely 'a home', 'medical', 'psychological support' and 'job assistance' is the need of the hour.

Are we sleepwalking to human catastrophe?
If not, let's wake up and save humanity from perennial agony.

www.ingramcontent.com/pod-product-compliance
Lightning Source LLC
Chambersburg PA
CBHW031538150726
47990CB00001B/221